I0457507

Doorways to the Unseen 2

6 Tales of Terror and Suspense

James Dermond

Ambages Books

This book is a work of fiction. The names, characters, organizations, places, events, and dialogue are either products of the author's imagination or are used in a fictitious manner.

Copyright © 2020 Ambages Books

All rights reserved.

No part of this publication may be reproduced or transmitted in any form or by any means, electronic or otherwise, without the express written permission of the publisher, with the exception of brief quotations used in book reviews.

ISBN 978-1-946038-01-2

Cover art by Jeff Purnawan

To the Dreamlands,

I may visit you yet

Contents

The Great Black Beast

I t was mid-summer when the procession appeared on the horizon. The men walked in a steady, solitary line over the rough road that stretched from the distant hillside to Mathilda and Hemma's remote village, nestled in the shaded valley. The penitents advanced under the early morning sun, their eremite leader chanting a monophonic hymn whose reply came in droning unison. They asked God to forgive them of their sins, to save them from further degradation, and to prevent the world from coming to an end while shrouded in these dark, uncertain times.

The origin of the pestilence was unknown, but it had spread with terrifying speed. First, it took the very old, then the very young; first lone travelers, then entire towns and cities; first the common folk, then the gentry and the clergy. The telltale black circles and weeping abscesses on the skin were followed by wracking coughs, violent convulsions, and then, lastly, death. The pestilence had no order, no reason—it sometimes struck down those previously healthy in only a few days, while others lingered for weeks before being consumed. No one knew whether they were to be the next victim.

When the band of penitents reached the village, they assembled in its square, surrounded by curious denizens.

The men removed their hoods and stripped their white-robed bodies to the waist. They then proceeded to flail their heavily scarred backs with knotted leather straps, still reciting their droning, hypnotic chant. The air around the villagers grew thick with the scent of freshly opened wounds and unwashed bodies; they breathed deeply of the penitents' mortified flesh . . .

Mathilda stood behind her younger sister Hemma, tightly gripping her arm. The girls' mother lay before them on a soaked bed fetid and rank with sickness; she had been stricken soon after the departure of the penitents. Greta had scarcely stirred that day. She had finally called her daughters to her and told them that she might not last the night. There was an errand, she said, that the sisters needed to complete for their mother once she had passed from this world.

"There will be no one in the village to care for you in less than a week's time." Greta's voice was thin, almost a whisper. "You must flee, or you will soon starve or be taken as well. The penitents! Only they could have brought this sorrow upon us."

This woman, with her sunken, pallid face and emaciated body, now seemed to her daughters a phantom, so distant from their once-vigorous mother. But as Greta spoke, a glimmer of her old self re-emerged for a scant moment: "Matthias will take you from here to my brother, Alarick. Alarick makes his home in seclusion near the untamed black forest. You must take something to him so your uncle will recognize you as his true kin."

Greta struggled to find the strength to sit up. Finally upright, she pointed to the stone-lined fireplace in the family dwelling's remaining room through the open door.

"Behind a loose stone under the mantle is a box with a pendant. I've kept it hidden there all these years. Even your father was ignorant of its secret place, God rest his soul.

Take it with you—keep it safe, and show it to Alarick when you find him. This pendant has been with my brother's family since before our own father's father was born."

Mathilda turned to the smoky kitchen outside the bedroom door and its now-cold fireplace, eyes settling on the ashes strewn about the hearth's interior.

Hemma was silent and did not look away from her mother. She looked for a moment, as if she were searching for something.

"Now go. It will take you less than a week if you trust in Matthias. Matthias pledged to care for you both as if you were his own flesh and blood. He promised me after Mathilda was born."

Her voice spent, Greta sank back into the bed's threadbare covers and closed her eyes. Her breath slowed, coming once again in shallow gasps. Mathilda followed Hemma to the fireplace, where her little sister was prying at a discolored stone. Mathilda closed the oaken door behind her. God willing, their mother would not suffer for much longer.

"Here it is," Hemma said, her voice flat.

Mathilda turned. Hemma was crouched by the fire, her small fingers scratched and covered with clay dust. The worn stone lay next to her on the kitchen's earthen floor. She reached into the newly formed hole and emerged with a compact, metallic box scarred from heat and blackened with soot. Slowly, Hemma opened the unlatched box.

Coming closer, Mathilda peered over her sister's shoulder. Inside the box rested a silvery pendant, strangely unmarred in contrast to its container. She leaned forward to take the pendant, but Hemma stopped her. "We need to fetch Matthias and start for Tüchingen," Hemma instructed. "Tüchingen is the last town before the forest. Matthias should be with the horses, as everyone else is gone."

And so the sisters left their home for the last time, bundling their few belongings into a sack that had been left by Matthias the previous day. The prospect of never seeing their mother again haunted Mathilda, but the idea of a new life waiting for her beyond their rustic settlement was enticing to her: a life beyond the ravages of the pestilence and the horrific memories of the past weeks.

Matthias was the village blacksmith, an imposing man who had learned the arts of the smithy from his father. As the rest of the villagers had succumbed or fled, Matthias had remained to tend to Greta's daughters. He had prayed that Greta might recover, but those prayers—to the angels and saints alike—had gone unanswered. Matthias knew he was fortunate to be alive and praised God for sparing him—and Greta's children, of course.

"We leave within the hour and will camp by the roadside at nightfall." He turned, fixing Mathilda with a hard look. "But know that the way between here and Tüchingen has become treacherous. With so few men-at-arms to keep them in check, bandits roam unchallenged." He shot Hemma a brief glance. Behind, the stable house's remaining horses whinnied gently. All but one would be left behind.

"Thank you, Master Matthias. May God bless you for your bravery and sacrifice." Mathilda reached forward to kiss Matthias' free hand, but he pulled away, seemingly embarrassed. The physical resemblance between Matthias and Mathilda was striking—both were tall, with a taut jawline set against fair features and clear blue eyes. Hemma's appearance, however, was so different from that of her older sister that one would hardly guess they were siblings. Hemma's dark brown eyes shone brightly on her foxlike face, and she wore her deep red hair in a long braid that ran down her back like a long tail.

Matthias secured the bridle around the dray horse's mouth and patted the animal's flank. Mathilda and Hemma seated themselves in the wooden cart harnessed behind the sturdy beast, resting against the packed supplies secured carefully against the elements. The mid-day sky was overcast; heavy rains would slow what would already be a lengthy journey over the failing country roads.

Matthias scrutinized his workhorse. "He may not be a Barbary, but he's as steady as God makes them." He turned and smiled slightly at his two passengers before climbing onto the cart's raised seat and taking hold of the horse's reins. *"Geschwinde Reise, meine Kinder,"* he said, pulling at the reins and urging the horse into an ambling trot.

The cart groaned over uneven earth, passing abandoned cruck houses plastered with wattle and daub, now silent as tombs. The dead were buried in a mass grave near a low, sloping hill just outside the village. Matthias had covered his hands and face with coarse cloth as he'd heaved his neighbors, then the village priest, then his aged parents, and finally his wife and two sons into the charnel pit. By the time the grave had begun to overflow, there was hardly a man left to seal it.

A light drizzle coated the trio as the storm clouds above them obscured the dim sun. The roads were empty, hushed, and devoid of souls as evening descended upon them. Matthias guided the cart to a clearing a hundred or so paces from the road, hiding the horse behind a cluster of trees and letting it feed on rich patches of wild grass. He covered the cart with sackcloth to protect it from the rain and then began to gather branches for the night's fire.

"We can only have a fire for so long. I don't want to risk attention from wandering cutthroats," Matthias said. The girls looked exhausted—even Hemma's bright eyes seemed dimmed, and Mathilda's fine blonde hair was plastered to her face.

Dinner was some barley bread and hard cheese. The small fire blazed and cast shadows about the travelers, heightening the sense of suffocation brought on by the inky blackness of the countryside.

"I'll wake soon. You and Hemma should sleep the whole night," Matthias said, not looking back at Mathilda. Instead, he bundled some birch saplings and lay back against them, propping himself into a sitting position. As the last waves of the fire's heat beat against his weathered skin, he allowed himself to doze off.

Hemma, stoic as always, had barely said a word since leaving the village, and now curled up for the night. Mathilda slowly fell into sleep, wrapping herself in the blankets Matthias had brought. As she closed her eyes, the dancing embers of the dying fire seemed to come alive, but only for a moment . . .

Low voices from the other room. Mathilda rose from the open cradle at the foot of her parents' bed and crept through the dark to the partially closed door leading to the kitchen. Rubbing her eyes, she peeked through—was that Mother in front of the hearth? With a man—a man who was not her father. Flames bathed the room in a ruddy glow, bright enough for Mathilda to pick out the outlines of the chthonian figures, shadows with no faces. Mathilda's father slumbered behind her in the bedroom.

"You must keep it. He'll never find it here," the man said, his voice taut and insistent. There was a soft grating sound as one of the fireplace's stones was removed from its spot. "The old fool won't even notice after we patch this up." The man was quite tall and shaggy, a mass of unruly hair hanging from his head and about his shoulders. Once the stone was back in place, the man reached down and grasped Mathilda's mother by the arms, pulling her in and kissing her with a hunger. Mathilda turned as she heard her father stir . . .

Mathilda woke to a morning that was cool and damp. A small ashen heap rested in front of her.

Matthias remarked as they set off again that the rain would probably get worse. Hemma sat across from Mathilda, her staid expression unchanged even as they crested bumps and gaping holes in the ill-maintained road to Tüchingen. They were closer now, making good progress despite the condition of the roadway.

Several successive nights passed uneventfully. When Matthias rose one morning, he looked overhead and saw what was coming. "There will be a torrential storm, probably later today. Let's try to cover as much ground as possible before it comes upon us." He nodded to Mathilda and gestured to the sack closest to him. "Take these to keep you dry. Your mother wanted you to have them."

Mathilda took out a long red cloak and a smaller black cloak which seemed as if it would fit Hemma. "Why red? Won't the bandits be able to see me from far away?"

"Just wear them," Matthias said. "We are not far from Tüchingen. We might even arrive late this eventide if the weather holds, which I fear it will not." He pulled at the horse's reins and the beast increased its gait, its pace now matching the sudden movement of the nimbus clouds hanging low in the sky overhead.

The rain started to pour late in the afternoon, quickly dousing the road in front of the cart. Mudflows formed, slowing the cart's advance and forcing Matthias to carefully navigate fresh pitfalls.

"Let's stop and find some shelter off the road!" Matthias shouted back to them, his voice lost in the downpour. "If we continue like this, we'll become stuck. This rain is making the road perilous." He tried to guide the cart to the roadside, looking for a safe spot among the mud and uneven terrain.

At once, the back of the cart lurched as the road beneath it abruptly gave way to mud. The cart's wheel sank, bringing the cart and its passengers to a halt. "By all the saints!" Matthias cried, "we'll not get the wheel out while these rains come down on us." He took a deep breath, bracing himself against the firm wood. "But I must try." He leaped from his perch on the cart, examined the stuck wheel, and then pushed from behind the cart in a vain attempt to free it.

Mathilda ushered her sister out of the cart. "Let us take the bags and stand outside the cart. Then Matthias might be able to get us loose." She was about to climb out when she felt Hemma tug at her cloak.

The girl was staring off into the mist. "Someone is coming," she said.

Mathilda followed her gaze, peering down the rain-drenched road. Hemma was right—a hobbled form was weaving toward them in an uncertain pattern. The figure was cloaked and carried no visible baggage.

"Matthias," Mathilda said, her eyes fixed on the figure. "Matthias!"

The smith turned from the mud-soaked wheel and stared at her. "What, girl?!"

When Mathilda didn't respond, he turned. The figure froze unexpectedly, as if waiting for Matthias.

Mathilda spoke in a muted tone: "Matthias, don't go. It may be a bandit. Let him come to us."

Matthias glanced over at Mathilda, wiped his wet brow with a cloth, and then began to move toward the figure, rain splattering over him.

Closer now, Matthias realized the stranger was a gnarled old man, most likely a beggar. The man pulled at the cowl of his cloak, hiding his face from view. Matthias was close enough to catch the faint hint of a putrescent odor, but the earthy scent of the falling rain quickly washed the smell from his nostrils.

The beggar croaked, "Alms, alms for the poor." He extended a filthy hand outward, palm up, from within the folds of his patchwork robe. Matthias took a few black pfennigs from his belt pouch and stepped forward, dropping the small coins into the beggar's soaked hand.

The beggar's voice changed, becoming a kind of low growl. "Thank you, kind sir," he said and bent forward as if to kiss Matthias' hand. Matthias pulled his hand away—but too late. The beggar lurched forward with a shocking swiftness and bit viciously into the thick flesh of Matthias' hand, the cowl of his cloak falling back.

Matthias let out a sharp cry, both from the pain and the sight now before him. The beggar's pitted face was that of a decaying corpse, enveloped in pus-filled, festering sores. Mathilda screamed as Matthias staggered back from the beggar, clasping his bloody hand. "My hand!" he cried, "it's burning!"

The beggar shambled away, madly cackling. "We are all lost! All the world's comin' to an end, it is. Judgment is upon us."

Mathilda ran to Matthias' side as the beggar disappeared into the nearby woods, concealed by the descending rain.

Black pools of water dotted the muddy roadway, reflecting the cart's wheels as it crawled past. The rain had ceased hours ago, and the sun was beginning to set over the horizon. Matthias struggled on, his skin ashen, hands barely holding the reins of the cart horse. He looked down and saw blood seeping out from under the cloth bandage covering his mangled hand. A blurred plain of swirling grey vectors, the world swam in front of him. His body shook.

Finally, he could go no further. Wincing, he turned back to the huddling children and, through a thin veil of perspiration, said, "Children, you must continue on without me. We are very close to Tüchingen. The road will have you there before nightfall if you make haste."

Mathilda had been crying quietly, and now the tears came in earnest. Hemma started to reach for their sack of belongings.

"What will become of you?" Mathilda wiped her face with her sleeve and looked up at Matthias.

"The pestilence will take me, most likely by dawn. I will rest by the side of the road, among those trees. Someone from Tüchingen should come back for the cart and the dray once I am gone. Go now—the hour is late."

Mathilda and Hemma walked briskly, their young legs unwearied. Evening came upon them quickly, and the road was soon illuminated by the bright full moon hanging prominently in the nocturnal firmament. The thatched roofs of Tüchingen's homes and shops became visible on the hillside, and the sisters began the steep path up to the town. Without Matthias, the girls would have to find their uncle Alarick's house alone.

Mathilda led Hemma through the deserted main street of the town and found the only building with visible lights, *The Lamb and Scythe*—a tavern. A weathered painted sign of a man holding a scythe and a lamb lilted in the nighttime breeze as the two girls entered through the creaking, iron-bound doorway.

The tumbling voices of townsfolk filled the tavern, as did the warmth of a roaring fireplace. The massive head of a black wolf was mounted prominently over the mantle.

"We are lost this night. We are looking for our uncle," Mathilda told the matron behind the bar.

The woman set down a platter of roasted game hens. She eyed the sisters suspiciously. "Why are two young girls traveling by themselves? Where is your father?"

"We come from Schwingheim. Our mother sent us to stay with our uncle." Mathilda feared the townspeople in Tüchingen might have heard of Schwingheim's sudden demise and believe that she and Hemma carried the pestilence, but she thought it unwise to lie.

The matron was taken aback. "My older brother married a girl and moved to Schwingheim many years ago. Once he moved away, we rarely saw him . . . that was before he went missing. Anselm had a daughter with his wife—Greta, her name was. The wife, I mean."

Mathilda swallowed. "My father's name was Anselm, and my mother's name is Greta. I never really knew him—he abandoned us when I was very young. Mother was already pregnant, and my little sister was born soon after."

A rough-looking man with the garb of a woodsman had been listening in and approached the bar. "That girl Anselm married wasn't from Tüchingen," he growled, eyes fixed on Mathilda. "Anselm never said where he met the girl. They were married in a rush, and he just left Tüchingen almost for good. We only saw him again a few times before he ran off, or whatever it was that happened to him."

He took a deep drink from his mug of ale. "Anyhow—Anselm wanted to move away from Tüchingen because of what happened to his young nephew. The boy was killed in front of most of the town . . . the Great Black Beast. It happened long ago, but I can still recall the Black Beast—its stench mainly—as if I had seen it just last night."

The man's eyes were haunted—even Mathilda, as young as she was, could see that. It was as if he was reliving a moment of terror kept buried for many years.

"In those days, packs of black wolves prowled the woods and fields around Tüchingen—the threat worsened with each passing year. The sheriff and his men promised to wipe the wolf packs out for good, but they were slow to do anything. So, some of the local men began hunting the wolves, journeying deeper into the Black Forest with each new hunting party. The hunters were making decent progress when the Great Black Beast struck for the first time."

The woodsman looked over at the matron, who returned his gaze with a pleading expression. He went on anyway: "A terrible storm had swept over the town, and the people sought shelter from the tempest. The church in Tüchingen is very old and built of quarry stone, so the town's families gathered inside to ride out the downpour and pray.

"The thunderstorm outside became very loud, almost deafening. The church shook, the timbers of its roof groaning under the storm. Children were crying, and everyone was huddled along the pews. The storm seemed to be reaching its peak when there was a howl that rose above the sound of the thunder—a howl of the likes I'd never heard, even from the savage wolves we'd hunted in the Black Forest.

"Many more howls answered it—and after barely a moment, the doors of the church burst open and a gigantic black thing loped in on all fours, rain falling all around it."

The man's eyes were wild, firelight flickering in the whites like dancing devils. "The thing looked like a huge wolf, but that wasn't what it was," he said, his voice hushed. "It was long, with thin legs and a hunched back, its mane of charcoal-black hair ending near the shoulders. The thing had a narrow snout but a wide face; it almost seemed like a man that had been twisted into the body of an animal.

"The Great Black Beast's eyes glowed red, and it bared its horrible fangs. Women started screaming as it ran along the church's nave, leaped forward, and grabbed Anselm's nephew by the throat. The beast shook the boy by the neck —blood was everywhere."

For a moment, he was still. Mathilda realized she hadn't been breathing.

"It dropped the dead boy and turned to find more prey—that was when the hunter, Wilhelm, shot it squarely in the face with his bow. The beast made the same blood-curdling howl we'd heard before and it fled, knocking over the priest's candle holders as it went."

The woodsman paused and collected himself, pressing his flinty fingers into tightly shut eyes. The tavern matron was silent, as if remembering that same night. The woodsman began to speak again, this time with even greater trepidation: "We prayed that we had seen the last of the Great Black Beast, but alas. It attacked again within a fortnight, carrying off a young girl. A hunting party was formed, this time with the sheriff and several deputies.

"The hunting party killed that wolf whose head now adorns this tavern, along with many other wolves—but none were the Black Beast. Over the next months, the wolves around Tüchingen were hunted to extinction, but there was never again any sign of that creature. It may have been driven into the furthest depths of the Black Forest. It could still be there today."

The woodsman gave Mathilda a hard stare. "You said you came from Schwingheim. How—"

But before he could continue, the tavern door slammed open and a young man in shepherd's clothes stumbled into the room. The man was breathing hard and paused, clutching at his chest. Finally, he heaved himself upright. Mathilda caught a glimpse of the dire look on his face.

"Squire Müller has taken ill!" he shouted to the room. "He shows the marks of the pestilence. They have locked him and his family inside their home and are going to set it ablaze this night!"

The townspeople stood from their tables and began to run for the door, shouting protests or encouragement; Mathilda wasn't sure which. Panic was about to seize Tüchingen, she knew, one that would set the townsfolk against each other.

The matron took Mathilda by the arm as the woodsman turned his back on them, heading for the tavern door. Mathilda and Hemma followed the woman into the tavern's deserted back kitchen and to a small postern door near some cupboards stacked high with kitchen wares. The matron pushed the door open, the moonlight revealing an expansive clearing and, at its edge, a wall of black and primeval trees.

"The burghers will blame new arrivals for what's about to happen. Seek out the safety of the Black Forest. Whatever waits for you there can be no worse than what will come upon Tüchingen by daybreak."

Mathilda peered into the woman's sweat-beaded face, itself bathed in the dull light of the kitchen's hearth. The woman closed the door without another word, and the sisters turned to peer up at the towering trees.

"Come on," Hemma said, and began walking into the woods.

A terse cough from the kitchen was the last sound they heard before the noises of the nighttime forest overtook them.

An enormous gleaming moon shone through the tops of the sheltering elm trees, the pearlescent centerpiece of a vast, star-filled sky. Mathilda and Hemma carried no torch or lantern, but the moonlight was bright enough for them to find a trail soon after venturing from Tüchingen.

Hemma turned as she crouched over a trail leading farther into the forest. "This one has been used recently," she said, "I can tell."

Mathilda stood over her sister, wearing a puzzled expression. "How would you know? Since when did you become a seasoned woodsman?"

"Trust me, I have a sense for such things. You'll know more in time."

Hemma led Mathilda along the indistinct path, careful to avoid the treacherous slopes and gullies along the way. Not long after, the girls stopped at the foot of an arching hill, its summit ensconced in a tangle of barren trees.

"Here. The trail stops here. There is a path to the top of the hill just ahead of us." Hemma pointed to a dirt track that wound up the side of the desolate hill and disappeared into the desiccated tree line.

"What do you think is up there? Somewhere we can stay the night?"

Hemma spoke over her shoulder as she climbed the path: "You'll find out."

The girls reached the end of the path and stood among the leafless trees. At the other end of the parched glade was a hovel, a solitary torch fixed to its front which lit the area against the intrusions of the surrounding forest.

Mathilda looked over at Hemma, who stared unblinking at the wood-and-clay structure. "Did you know this was here?"

"Let's go inside," Hemma said, walking ahead.

Mathilda hesitantly followed, unsure of what she had been led into by her sister.

A single knotted wood door with a low arched top appeared to be the only means of entry into the hovel, its side walls obscured by flanking trees. The tar-pitch torch burned next to the entryway from its ornate metal sconce, which contrasted sharply with the otherwise impoverished home. Hemma held out a closed fist, paused, and then knocked twice in succession.

There was a stirring behind the door, and then someone called, "Who's there? Who disturbs me?" The voice was unpleasant, harsh.

Hemma called back, "We seek shelter for the night. The forest is not safe, and we ask for reprieve."

After a moment, the door swung inward. A tall, gaunt man wearing a bristling black beard and long, unruly hair streaked with gray stooped in the entryway. He stared at the girls briefly without an utterance and then gestured. "Come inside."

Hemma followed the man into his home while Mathilda stood next to the burning torch, assessing their situation. She swallowed the lump in her throat and tentatively followed her sister into the dimly lit room. She had no other choice.

The hovel's interior was warm and hazy, with a bubbling stew pot resting on a tripod over the fireplace's hearth. Smoke from the fire wafted up the stone chimney, but some of the vapors failed to escape and instead hung over the room. Mathilda coughed as she and Hemma were ushered into wooden chairs beside a crude table.

The man stood over them. "I never have visitors, not in these woods. Where are you children from? What are your names?" He looked at them sternly but did not seem menacing.

"I am Mathilda, and this is my little sister, Hemma. We come from Schwingheim."

The man at first said nothing, but then his demeanor changed, becoming more animated. "Such a long way to travel for two young girls. Are you perhaps looking for someone?"

Hemma reached across the table and touched Mathilda's arm. "Show him the box."

Mathilda looked back at Hemma; somehow, she did not feel as if she could refuse. She reached into her cloak and produced the metal case they had brought from their mother's hiding place. Hesitantly, she prised open the lid and placed the box on the table.

Immediately, the man became agitated, visibly excited. He took the silver pendant from the box and held it across a lank hand, examining it with a sly, wolfish grin. "Oh yes, this. This," he said, nearly panting in anticipation.

The pendant hanging from the chain was an argent coin of ancient design, its relief the image of a she-wolf suckling cubs. The man grabbed its case from the table and put the pendant back inside. "I will keep this for you. It's a valuable item," he said, looking down at Mathilda. "But you must be hungry. Let's have some supper."

The man and the sisters ate hot stew. After, he prepared two cots for them in a spare room at the hovel's rear. Mathilda was unsettled by the night's events but was weary too; besides, she did not want to pull Hemma away to sleep outside. Was this man Uncle Alarick? He hadn't told them his name—not even when he'd bid the girls goodnight.

Mathilda sat up suddenly, squinting into the dark, windowless room, the last dying embers from the crackling fireplace the only light. Hemma was gone. Her cloak was neatly folded on her cot, but there was otherwise no sign of her.

Rising quickly, Mathilda wrapped herself in her cloak before stepping out into the main area of the hovel. The man was nowhere to be seen. Mathilda opened the front door and walked outside; the pristine moon still shone like noon, illuminating her steps as she followed a trail past the hovel and farther up the hillside, deeper into the forest.

The barren trees parted and revealed a clear path to a hill that looked down over the hovel. In the shrouded distance, a bonfire blazed. Mathilda approached—figures moving became apparent, murky silhouettes swaying as if in dance.

Mathilda stopped not far from the fiercely burning fire, within sight of Hemma and Alarick. Both were naked, along with a score of bare-skinned, feral people who were falling onto their hands and knees. Alarick hung the silvery pendant around Hemma's neck and Hemma dropped to the ground with a snarl, reddish fur sprouting from her back, her hands becoming paws.

Alarick extended his arms to the brilliant starry tapestry above him and arched his back as if in ecstasy. The wolf pack around the bonfire let out a chorus of bloodthirsty howls as the Great Black Beast rose on its four grotesque legs, its slavering jaws glittering with razor-sharp fangs.

The black beast howled joyously and, all at once, Mathilda understood.

The Devil's Garden

There was no light in the coffin, and not much more air. Clarence writhed in the tight, confined space as he surfaced suddenly into horrible consciousness. At once, he pulled his leaden arms from his sides and onto his chest and began pressing against the lid of the coffin with the palms of his hands, becoming more frantic with each faltering push. His own jagged, raspy breath was the only sound Clarence could hear over the cracking of his fingernails as they broke into the overhead enclosure of his buried prison.

Splinters of pine fell onto his parched mouth and forehead, threatening to slip into his eyes. Searing pain bit into him as his fingertips shredded against the wood, with thin streams of blood running over his hands and onto his face. Despite the total blackness of the coffin, Clarence sensed his vision was clouding with each halting, panicked breath. How much time did he have left?

There were muffled noises above him. The garbled intonation of men speaking and then a commotion of vigorous, hurried digging. Clarence paused and lay still, trying to preserve his last remaining breaths. As he drifted into unconsciousness, a shovelhead broke through the wood coffin lid, and a flood of humid, tropical air rushed over him . . .

The window of his fourth-floor hotel room was unlatched and open, offering Clarence a late-night view of the city and its port.

At once, he sprang up in bed, crying out. Nothing—there was nothing. It had just been a dream. He exhaled, perched on the edge of the mattress, and sucked in a deep, deliberate breath. The sheets were damp with sweat, the night's moist air hanging over him.

The nightmare had returned, and so soon after the last one. Each time, Clarence dreamed of being buried alive and then dug up by some unknown interlopers. Yet it was the immediacy of this most recent burial ordeal that surprised him; his passenger ship had docked on the island only this past morning, and this frightful vision of vivisepulture had invaded his dreams the very same night.

The recurring nightmare had been with Clarence since he'd first landed on this ill-fated island several years prior, but tonight's episode had been the most vivid yet. He always got a sense that the burial was occurring somewhere on the island itself, but so little could be grasped from the dream—there was just a dark coffin, his terror at being buried alive, and the men breaking in with a shovel just before he awoke.

Clarence poured tepid water from the pitcher on the worn table across from his bed. He refilled the pitcher and washed his stubbled face before drying himself with a rough cloth. The ceramic toilet set and the ornately carved table had seen better days, but still retained some of their original colonial elegance. Few visitors came to this island, but those who did most often sought their fortunes—even at the risk of their lives.

The early morning bustle on the street outside the hotel stirred Clarence from the shallow, fitful sleep he'd found after waking from the nightmare. He was to meet a man at *Café la Plantation* to discuss the shipping of contraband goods off the island. The coastal city on the other side of the calm, green-blue sea was the goods' destination.

The island was a haven for sellers of illicit cargo, possessing little in the way of effective government and even less in the way of law enforcement. The last of the occupying foreign soldiers were leaving the island for good and, in their absence, a void of any unifying authority.

Clarence stood in front of the oval floor mirror resting on an upright frame near the room's door. He'd not bothered shaving, and had dressed in a white summer suit and straw boater hat. He adjusted a silk necktie under his pressed shirt collar.

The faint dark circles under his eyes betrayed Clarence's sleeplessness, but he hoped Junior wouldn't notice. He and Junior had done business on several occasions, and it was Clarence's heartfelt wish this would be the last time he would make the journey to the island.

The handful of runs Junior had conducted with Clarence had always been from the eastern part of the island, which was a separate, autonomous nation unto itself. If the pending deal with Junior was closed, it would set Clarence up in relative comfort, and he could abandon the smuggling life for some less risky line of work.

The mirror's glass was very polished, in sharp contrast to the otherwise dingy hotel room. This cheval mirror might have even been lifted at some point from one of the many ruined plantations in the island's interior.

Giving himself one final glance over, Clarence reached out to touch the glass. His reflection distorted as the mirror began to tilt upward. He looked down as it pivoted toward him and saw his reflection, now a mass of liquescent flesh, tumorous and suppurating, crawling with turgid maggots.

Clarence grasped the border of the mirror and held it tightly, staring into the silvery glass. The horror was gone; his face's reflection was finely wrinkled and weathered but hale, as it had been only a moment before.

A chill came over Clarence as he thought on the repulsive visage. "Nerves, that's all it was," Clarence assured himself, "bad dreams are chasing me even into daytime. A shot of vermouth at *Café la Plantation* will do me good."

The street outside the hotel was filled with vendors, men pushing produce carts, and women carrying baskets on their heads. The scent of ripe fruit mixed with the foul air of the city washed over Clarence as he stepped out, the fetid aroma accentuated by the humid climate. *Café la Plantation* was but a few city blocks over from the hotel.

"In dollars, not francs, like you asked." Clarence placed the dull brown paper envelope on the café table and grabbed a peeling wooden chair from nearby, seating himself across from Junior.

"And good day to you as well, Clarence. Where are your manners?" Junior said in heavily accented English. He smiled broadly, quickly reaching across the table and stuffing the envelope into his pants pocket, glancing around the café as he did so.

Clarence replied, "*Bonjour, Monsieur* Junior. You look well. The molasses trade must have been good to you of late, especially now prohibition is done."

Junior wrinkled his forehead and leaned into the table. "*Monsieur* Clarence, I have to say, I'm surprised to see you back. Maybe the money was just too good to pass up, no?"

Clarence recalled his first meeting with Junior and the dangerous runs they had completed together: moving alcohol and sugarcane molasses to the mainland at great risk to their safety and the lives of their crew. Junior had guts, but Clarence had never fully learned to trust him, and now was no exception.

Junior had been born and raised on the island but had learned English from "your army men and a missionary schoolteacher." He was a young man, vigorous and self-assured, but always cloaked in uncertainty; Junior was a wild card even among the tumultuous environs of the island. Clarence still did not even know Junior's given name, as he had never revealed it.

Clarence looked directly at Junior. "Like you, I'm getting squeezed by the new laws on booze. Why would someone buy from us when it's now legal and on the shelves again? But we can still undercut the competition on molasses; no tariffs, no taxes, so lower prices for our customers. This is a buy I can't pass up."

A waiter came to their table and Clarence ordered a shot of vermouth.

Junior waited for the waiter to leave before leaning back in his seat and grinning. "We'll meet tonight at the docks not far from here and take an old tug up the coast. The loading place is in a jungle spot I've used before, where no one will look for us. The streets will be empty—this is the first night of the Feast of Souls. Everyone will be inside their homes or at the cemeteries, so you don't have to worry about being followed.

"The whole cargo will be placed on your sea-worthy ship and, from there, you can take it back home. Your crew will be on that ship, *Monsieur* Clarence?"

Clarence nodded, trying to keep his face unreadable. "They were paid in part before I left and will be there. Just a skeleton crew—after all, we want to involve as few as possible. I'm much more careful now than I was in the past. Your people will supply the labor to load the goods, I take it?"

Junior's face twitched, but before he could speak, the waiter returned. He took a crystal shot glass from his tray and placed it in front of Clarence before turning and departing.

"Yes, *Monsieur* Clarence," Junior said, his composure restored, "you don't worry about that. Our men will never breathe a word, I promise you. See you at nine o'clock."

Clarence walked back to his hotel, feeling a bit lighter now that the first part of his last trip was done. The taste of the vermouth lingered in his mouth, and now he needed some breakfast. The hotel had a small dining room where he could get a plate of eggs with plantains. The late morning and afternoon would provide the time for Clarence to read the sale papers he had brought with him and plot out what would happen to this sizable shipment once he was back in port.

The morning and afternoon passed quickly. Clarence spent the time working at the table in his room and had lunch brought up to him from the hotel kitchen. Papers were spread over the makeshift desk, with his open leather journal displaying the figures he had calculated and jotted down. Junior had received the advance payment, and the rest would be paid to the smuggling crew's captain once Clarence took possession of his cargo.

He finished what was left of his lunch for supper and then prepared to go down to the docks to meet Junior. The late autumn sun was beginning to set over the horizon and rosy-fleeced light spilled in through the open window of his hotel room. Clarence sat on his bed and looked out over the city and to the sea beyond it, knowing it would soon be dark. The streets would be deserted, just as Junior had said— tonight was the first night of the festival.

"Will you be back soon, *Mesye*?" The woman at the hotel's front desk said as Clarence walked by her station. "Tonight's not a good night to be out on those streets, especially for a Yankee. Why don't you just get some sleep instead?"

Clarence could see the young woman was genuinely concerned, so he stopped and shot her a reassuring smile. "A friend told me there's a festival tonight, a feast for the dead. I'd heard about it during other visits, but I was never here when the festival took place. People were always reluctant to speak of what went on. I'm eager to see what all the fuss is about."

From here, the streets outside appeared pitch black, with no signs of lights from other buildings or passersby. The weather had cooled, a balmy breeze wafting through the hotel's yellow-painted double doors and over Clarence and the young woman. She leaned forward from the check-in counter, her long, curly, reddish hair loose, spilling down her heavily freckled face. Her expression was now quite anxious.

"You are right, *Mesye*. It is the *Fet Gede*, the night when the world of the dead and the world of the living are closest. During the day, the people were in the streets, but now they are seeing their families who have passed on. But who knows who is out there? I tell you, it's not safe."

"Restless spirits?" Clarence was just about able to hide his amusement. "I'm just meeting someone. I'll stick to the main thoroughfare as a precaution. But thanks for your concern; I appreciate it."

Despairing, the woman breathed in a hoarse whisper, "It's the *Culte des Mortes, Mesye. Jaden Dyab la a*. The Devil's Garden. Stay away from the graveyards this night and the next, no matter who invites you there. I will pray that *les Saints Bénis* keep you."

Clarence gave her a final confused smile before turning and sauntering out onto the empty street of the hotel district. The woman watched him go, her sad eyes boring into his back until, at last, the darkness swallowed him.

JAMES DERMOND

The hard-packed dirt streets of the city were ill-maintained, but an extensive tram system ran through the downtown area and its adjacent districts, which belied the abject poverty of the capital and of the island itself. The public trams had ceased running several hours ago, and Clarence proceeded on foot to his appointment with Junior.

Single lights, probably candles, flickered in the open windows of tenement homes, but otherwise, the streets were sheltered in darkness. The moon was only a waning crescent but provided most of the remaining illumination from its perch in the cloudy night sky. In the distance, Clarence spied a long procession of lights advancing in single-file out of the city, but he was too far away to make out any more than that.

Turning a street corner, Clarence was nearing his destination. The waterfront had recently undergone new construction, and a concrete wharf had been added, which extended ahead of the antiquated wooden docks built during the city's founding. As he paused in front of a dilapidated shipwright's warehouse near the open avenue, a shadow cast itself over him, seemingly from nowhere.

Clarence looked around and saw nothing. The street was quiet and empty. He took out a packet of *Gaulois Bleu* from his coat's front pocket and lit one with his silver lighter, taking a long drag before continuing on. Only moments later, he paused again, a shadow casting itself into his path, this time from behind. It was larger now, and it had a shape: the shape of a man.

Clarence turned and again saw nothing. Did someone know about his meeting with Junior? Perhaps a rival smuggler? Clarence never carried a weapon—he had always feared arrest more than robbers—but now, and not for the first time, he regretted being without a gun.

Spinning back around, he hurried on, pulling his jacket tight around him despite the warm evening. The nighttime sea stretched out to his right, its cresting waves glimmering in the faint moonlight, and he traced a route along the edge of the water by the docks. The docks were destitute, the cluster of ships parked in the city's harbor without occupants. If someone was planning on attempting to waylay him, he would have to make a run for the hotel, which was now blocks away.

There was someone in the distance. A figure stood near a tugboat moored to the dock, their features not yet visible in the dim light. The boat bobbed slightly in the warm sea wind, and Clarence hurried his step. An enormous shadow spread itself across his path as he moved, the outline of the figure's top hat and long-sleeved coat now clear. Clarence froze and stared at the animated silhouette which abruptly gestured to him, tipping its hat and then waving a hand in a gesture of farewell.

The shadow receded behind a stack of shipping crates and barrels, slowly retreating from Clarence's view. When he looked up, he found Junior walking toward him.

"*Monsieur* Clarence, what is that expression on your face? You see your dead papa or something?" Junior's smirk was obvious even in the low light.

"I . . . I just saw a man. I think he was following me." Clarence felt uneasy, steadying himself as he tossed his spent cigarette butt into the gently churning waves splashing up against the mooring poles.

"There is no man, Clarence. No one is here. Just us and the souls of the dead who roam this night. Let's get on the boat; the crew is waiting."

Clarence quickly scanned the docks before following Junior down the boarding ramp and onto the tugboat. The boat's captain was behind the tug's helm, but none of the other crewmen showed themselves.

Junior unmoored the tug from the docks, throwing the length of rope back onto the ramp as the captain nodded and started the boat's engine. The engine sputtered and convulsed for a moment before chugging along at an even pace. At last, the tug drifted away from the docks and out to sea, gaining speed as the harbor grew smaller. Once they were past the city's limits, they made a hard turn toward the shore.

The tugboat parted the murky waters, white-capped frothing waves breaking from its port and starboard sides. The tug's destination was a remote and mostly uncharted jungle clearing near the island's sparsely populated interior.

The night sky had become clear, and Clarence stood at the tugboat's bow, gazing up into the starry canopy above him, nearly lost in thought. He heard Junior say something to the captain from the bridge behind him, but the chugging of the tug's engine drowned out the words.

"There are no excuses! You men are just lazy rats."

The four crew members stared up at Clarence sullenly as he berated them.

"We're behind schedule now, because of this." Clarence stood in front of the men as the sun began to set over the sea behind him, looking down at them from the chartered merchant ship's main hatch. Clarence had hired the ship and its crew to transport this run of illicit goods from the island, but the ship's captain wasn't entirely clear on the nature of the cargo.

Normally a very silent man, the ship's first mate spoke up. "We only did as you asked us. You were wrong about how long loading the ship would take. There was more cargo than what was written on the shipper's ledger." The first mate was an experienced seaman—taciturn, rough, and haggard—but was articulate in his own way.

Clarence sighed, his anger dissipating. "I went by what the suppliers' estimate. Now let's get this finished and be on our way. I'm losing money as we bicker over this mess." Clarence stepped down and walked away, ignoring the glare the first mate gave him as he descended the ship's stairs to his quarters below deck.

This was not the first time Clarence had spoken harshly to the crew; he and the captain had maintained a working relationship that had lasted several years. Clarence had cultivated a reputation for callousness, even cruelty, among the captain's sailors, and the men had quickly grown to resent him. This commercial ship had run most of his biggest jobs from the island during prohibition.

The chartered ship would leave port that evening on a voyage due to last almost a week. The trip would end with a late-night docking in the waters outside the discharge port. The cargo would then be transported to shore on smaller, more nimble vessels so the goods could evade customs. Clarence wasn't sure if the ship's crew knew the value of the cargo they were carrying, but the ship's captain was a long-time retainer, and Clarence believed he could be trusted.

There was a knock at the cabin door. "Clarence, may I have a word with you?" It was the gruff voice of the ship's captain.

"Please, come in," Clarence replied without rising from his desk.

The door opened and the captain entered, his bearded face shadowy in the low light of the Bakelite desk lamp. "The men are becoming angry and frustrated," the captain announced. "First Mate Dorman came to me and said they are being overworked. That you are pushing them too hard to make an impossible schedule." The captain was an older man who'd spent many years at sea, and often left Clarence to supervise the crew while they loaded and unloaded his goods.

"Not true at all, Captain Hancock," was Clarence's measured response. "It's the men's fault we're behind as they didn't follow the schedule. If we're late to the offshore meet-up point, the handlers won't be there with the boats. No boats, no way to get the cargo to shore. We'd have to turn around and go back out to sea."

Captain Hancock stepped back and seemed to be weighing something up in his head. Clarence knew he was a valuable client and that the captain knew a serious disagreement with him might very well lead to his business being taken elsewhere. "I'll see what

I can do with the men. You're right—we can't miss the drop-off point or it will cost us all."

The captain tipped his peaked cap to Clarence and then slowly closed the cabin door. The muffled sound of the captain's footsteps echoed from the stairwell and then, for a few moments, from the deck above. Clarence sat and stared at the closed door as the footsteps faded, returning to the task at hand only once they were gone.

With his bookkeeping ledgers open in front of him, Clarence noted with satisfaction that this shipment of rum, molasses, and spices would be his most lucrative yet. The final sale of these goods would elevate Clarence's smuggling business into a new class of operation. He would no longer need to retain Captain Hancock with his aging watercraft and surly crew; he would be able to afford a ship of his own and his own men. Clarence wondered with some amusement whether Captain Hancock's crew were tempted to mutiny, given how large a sum of money was involved in this transaction. Did Hancock's men understand the full worth of what was being shipped?

The sound of footsteps and a hurried knock abruptly broke Clarence's stream of thought. A voice spoke from the other side of the cabin door: "We are docking to refuel, Mr. Morris. Please come above deck in fifteen minutes."

Clarence stood and rushed to open the door. A young man—a member of the crew—stood in front of him.

"Fifteen minutes, sir. We need to stop before going out to sea."

Clarence gripped the edge of the open door in frustration. He sputtered angrily, "There was no scheduled stop. Who approved this?"

The crewman replied, "First Mate Dorman, sir. We didn't have time to refuel due to all hands on the loading dock, so we are stopping now."

Slamming the door without a word, Clarence returned to his desk. He gathered his business papers and put them into the desk's top drawer, locking the drawer with the small key he kept on a chain around his neck. Clarence glanced at his reflection in the cabin's framed wall mirror and placed his straw boater hat on his head. As he turned his back on the mirror to leave, a caliginous shape, darkling and nebulous, began to form within the mirror's surface.

The ship had made slow progress along the island's coast and was now far from a port of any size. Clarence stood on the upper deck and gazed out at the sea, its waves sparkling in the bright moonlight of the evening. Their modestly sized steamship was headed toward a set of wooden piers, exhaust smoke trailing from its twin funnels. The piers protruded into the shallow waters of the jungle's shoreline; standing atop them were several men who appeared to be waiting for them.

The ship docked, and the men began moving barrels from the adjacent pier to the ship: fuel for the oil-fired steam boilers. Clarence saw that Captain Hancock and First Mate Dorman were already on the shore, moving between tents pitched in the clearing and speaking with some of the local men. Clarence walked up the two makeshift planks connecting the ship to the pier and sought out the clump of tents nestled at the fore of the jungle's tangled undergrowth.

"Come sit with us, Clarence. Armand here is going to share some of his spiced rum." Captain Hancock was in a jovial mood; he seemed a different man to the old captain who'd questioned Clarence earlier. Clarence seated himself on one of the folding canvas chairs in front of the camp's main tent, between the captain and first mate.

The captain placed a coarse hand on Clarence's shoulder, reassuring him. "Our ship should be ready within the hour, and you can get some rest after a nightcap. Here, drink up." The young man Captain Hancock had introduced as Armand handed Clarence a drink in a glass tumbler.

"Thanks," offered Clarence as he took his first shallow sip from the green enameled tumbler. Strong stuff—the spice was almost cloying to Clarence's palate.

Clarence studied the campsite beyond the open fire, the only source of light nearby besides the oil lamps that hung from posts *dotting the camp. Some of the laborers were standing nearby, restless and shifty. Clarence took another drink from the tumbler, noting Captain Hancock was holding an empty glass.*

"Mr. Morris, you seem sleepy. Why don't you finish your rum and then head to the ship? We'll be embarking soon." First Mate Dorman hovered near Clarence's chair. His voice was acerbic, almost mocking in tone, his timeworn features hollow in the light of the flickering flames.

Clarence put the tumbler to his lips, but it fell from his hand, the remaining rum spilling out over his clothes. He tried to stand but felt dizzy, dropping back onto the flimsy chair behind him. Slowly, he slid onto the sandy ground.

He felt hands take hold of his deadened limbs, lifting him up . . .

But what happened next? Clarence looked away from the tugboat's bow and up into the late-night sky again, as if waking from a trance. Junior called to him: "*Monsieur* Clarence, the captain wishes to have a word with you."

The times that followed that night at the camp had not been good ones. Clarence never recovered his cargo, which set him back years financially. His succeeding memory was of wandering along a deserted beach in the early morning, his mouth and skin parched, his white suit soiled and torn.

Clarence had found his way from the beach to a small town several miles away and hitched a ride on a cart back to the city. Days had passed unaccounted for. Accepting a loan from a business associate, Clarence purchased a ticket on a steamer headed home. He never saw Captain Hancock or his crew again.

The isolated cove consisted of a natural clearing in the jungle, a white sandy beach, and a single but sturdy pier lit by hanging lanterns extending out into the littoral waters. The tugboat docked, and Junior roped it securely to its moorings. Clarence stepped from the creaky deck onto the pier from a raised plank and peered around. The sandy beach was empty, but a trail led off into the jungle from which flickering lights were visible.

Clarence hadn't seen anyone else on the tug besides Junior and the tug's captain. Also, where were his hired ship and its crew?

Turning, Clarence saw Junior disappearing down the trail and into the jungle. The outline of his moving form was barely visible against the shelter of the tree ferns and tall hardwoods lining the pathway. Clarence stepped onto the stretch of fine sand in front of him, crossing the threshold from the shore to the jungle clearing, and then stepped onto the trail, following Junior.

The tropical forest around him was very active, humming with the ambient nighttime sounds of insect life. Clarence stopped to remove his boater hat and wipe the accumulated sweat from this brow. Where was Junior? He could no longer see him up ahead.

He emerged onto another clearing surrounded by jungle, lit only by a small bonfire at its center. As Clarence approached, erratic shadows danced in the grass, and large, exaggerated shapes loomed amid the trees.

Clarence saw a line of ragged men lifting crates and barrels onto a series of rolling flatbed carts, the carts having been perhaps retrieved from some derelict railway station. The men's actions were stiff and awkward, their steps mechanical and halting. As Clarence drew closer, he could see all of them were very gaunt, with sunken eyes and ashen complexions.

There was a rustling noise from among the ferns close to the trail. From behind Clarence, another of the gaunt men trod out of the jungle, his pallid face impassive and unblinking. Without noticing Clarence, he shambled past him across the clearing and took up the trail's path, which continued at the clearing's far side. The macabre figure was carrying something—it laid across his outstretched arms.

Clarence watched the gaunt man for a brief time before following at a distance behind him. Maybe, he reasoned, the man would lead him to Junior.

The trail snaked through the dense jungle, leading up a shallow hill and then back down again to the jungle floor. Upon descending, Clarence saw the crumbling edifice of a once-stately plantation, its former palatial splendor evident even now.

The gaunt man made his way up the vine-strewn steps of the plantation's columnated exterior and then through its partially open doors, vanishing from view. Clarence paused at the base of the hill and examined the grand building. The broken windows of both floors showed no light within; only the muted illumination of the crescent moon through the jungle canopy revealed any details of the abandoned dwelling.

Clarence hurried across the half-buried cobblestone path to the wide double doors. He pushed inside and paused at the foot of a blighted imperial staircase. Clarence could see the plantation house had indeed been a grand château for its master—gilded portraits hung on every wall, and a ballroom adjacent to the foyer stretched off into shadow. Clarence listened for the sound of footsteps, but none could be heard.

He eased past the cracked rococo doors of the ballroom. In its center stood a strange thing: a large cheval mirror, very similar to the one in his hotel room but much heavier and of more elaborate design. Resting about the mirror were many fetishes and unlit votive candles, black and sickly in color. The mirror was both repulsive and attractive at once, and Clarence was drawn toward it.

"There you are, *Monsieur* Clarence. We've been waiting for you."

Clarence turned sharply to see Junior stepping out of the shadows of the ballroom's interior. His face was painted chalky white, with thick black lines framing his eyes and mouth.

The votive candles surrounding the mirror flared and began burning brightly, revealing the other men who had formed a wide ring around Clarence. The men's faces were painted in the same ritual fashion as Junior's, the make-up resembling a kind of death mask. They stood silently, as if waiting for someone's arrival.

Distant drums began to beat somewhere outside, their rhythms swelling and rising. Clarence eyed the men assembled before him, licking his lips and trying to count them—fifteen maybe, or more. At once, he bolted, barreling past Junior, but two men—God, they were fast—seized him by the arms and dragged him back. They threw him down before the mirror, in which a shape as black as a funeral pall was now forming.

Looking away, Clarence shut his eyes and clasped his ears to shield them from the manic cadence of the rising drums. The sound grew louder, filling the space of the gutted ballroom. Clarence gasped, sweat beading on his skin, his head jerking in a panicked spasm toward the mirror as an enormous shadow cast itself between him and this portal to the world of the dead.

Junior spoke in a clear, powerful voice: "Papa called you back from across the sea, Clarence. That is why you were having those dreams. Your men betrayed you, gave you to Papa to make into one of his servants. You came to your senses once you were pulled out of the ground, and you got away. No one's ever done that before, I'll give you that.

"But now you are here, and Papa will collect what is his on this night, the night when the world of the dead and the world of the living are closest."

Clarence panted and gulped, his terror tightening in his throat. Then, finding the strength to speak, he shouted above the din of the drums, "What is his? What of mine is Papa's?"

Junior smirked and then nodded toward the mirror. "Why, your soul, *Monsieur* Clarence. Papa wants your soul."

A pair of massive arms reached out of the mirror, stygian as the night, and seized Clarence around the waist.

Clarence let out a scream, its sound nearly drowned out by the wildly thrashing drums, his body pulled into the mercury surface of the mirror. He seemed to melt away piece by piece, until only a single straining hand remained, clawing at nothing. Soon, that too disappeared into the netherworld of the mirror.

Far-off cries echoed from somewhere, and at once, the beating drums fell silent. Junior stepped toward the now-dormant mirror, touching his fingers to the glass.

The gaunt men labored near the spent bonfire, having worked throughout the night. Their task was almost done, and rays of morning sunlight were scattered through the giant fronds of the tree ferns sheltering the jungle clearing. The cargo was assembled, loaded onto the flatbed carts; it was almost ready to be pushed across the long trail of wooden planks set back to the beach. A newly arrived commercial steamer was docked at the pier.

Junior stood at the planks' end, where the sandy beach met the pier. He lit a *Gauloises* taken from a packet in his pocket and adjusted the straw boater hat on his head. The steamer's captain walked up the ramp from his ship and raised an arm in greeting.

"Good morning," the captain called out. "What a night it was! We were well ahead of schedule when a terrible storm came out of nowhere." The captain was young but was not a novice seaman. He and his crew had been badly shaken by a ferocious tempest which had beset them the previous night, the likes of which they had never seen before.

Junior flashed a grin. "Strange—we waited for you, but you never came. The sea was peaceful at these shores, like the way I sleep at night." He ambled his way across the planks to join the captain on the pier.

The captain eyed Junior as he approached, frowning slightly. "Even our radio signal was jammed. The waters to these ports are usually so calm, like you said, but we were tossed on the waves for hours. I was sure we were done for when the storm just rolled back, almost as quickly as it had come, exactly at midnight." Removing his seaman's cap for a moment, the captain wiped his brow with a cloth he kept in his trouser pocket, the heat from the island's morning sun already bearing down on him.

Junior held his lit cigarette between two fingers and offered the captain one, which the man accepted. "Mr. Morris had to leave very early this morning," Junior said. "Business matters that couldn't wait another day. We'll load the steamer's hold with his cargo, and you can be on your way."

The captain nodded, took a shaky puff from the *Gauloises*, and, without a word, turned to walk back down the ramp to the deck of his ship. Junior strolled along the planks to the hidden clearing in the jungle and found his older brother, Armand, at work. Armand was herding the ghastly troupe of laborers back into the plantation house where the steamer's crew wouldn't see them. He and Junior would then push the full carts to the pier and help the crew unload the cargo.

"Hey, Bénison, where you get the *blanc* from?" Armand gestured toward one of the gaunt men shuffling near the end of the line. The man had the same withered countenance and vacant, staring eyes as the others, but seemed out of place among the workers. His skin was particularly pale, and he wore a tattered white suit coat which had once clearly been a piece of fine clothing.

Junior replied, "Oh, just someone who owed Papa a debt." He then grinned devilishly. "A debt which has now been repaid."

A God in a Grotto

Abigail stood at the door to her father's study, her breath coming in short, nervous bursts. She glanced over the ornate carvings in the door's sash, all of which depicted pastoral scenes from the English countryside.

There were images of woods and valleys, shepherds with their flocks, birds in the fields and meadows, and a hunter arching his bow. A ram's head was prominently displayed at the top of the dark mahogany door's solid frame, its curving horns projecting in relief. The rustic scenes were exceptionally detailed, and the door frame was likely older than Abigail's family's home in Wiltshire.

Abigail paused and then rapped on the study door.

"Come in," she heard her father's voice answer in reply.

She cautiously opened the door. Inside, her father was seated at his writing desk, his back to the door. She spoke in her soft child's voice: "Father, Mother said you wanted to see me."

Father turned around to face her, the light of the afternoon sun filtering through the study's partially curtained bay window. "Yes, Abigail, please come in. Come here and stand next to my desk."

Abigail did as she was told. Placed on Father's writing desk among his journals and loose papers was a bell-shaped glass display case resembling the cloches Abigail's mother used in the family garden.

Smiling pleasantly, Father said, "I have something to show you." He lifted the glass dome from its base and took a polished stone, blood-red in color, into the palm of his hand. He held out the stone in front of Abigail, as if offering it to her.

Abigail had always felt apprehension whenever she visited Father's study and personal library, which was not very often. The study was a forbidden place to the rest of the family; Arthur Barrett had always told his daughters to never enter this room without permission. Since the door to the study was nearly always kept locked, Abigail often wondered how he thought she or Evelyn would get in even if they wanted to.

Father closed his fingers tightly around the stone and then squeezed for several moments, all the while wearing a curious expression. When Father relaxed his fingers and displayed the contents of his open palm, a small grey toad rested there. The toad turned in Father's palm and gulped, but made no attempt to leap from its perch onto the study's floor.

Quickly grasping Abigail's right arm, Father deposited the live toad into her palm with his free hand. "Squeeze tightly, Abigail," he murmured. "Don't be afraid; you won't hurt him."

An impassive Abigail did as her Father asked.

"Now, open your hand and look," Father instructed.

Abigail slowly relaxed her fingers from her palm, extending them outward. The polished bloodstone from the display case was in her hand, the toad gone.

Father removed the stone from Abigail's hand and returned it to the display case on his desk. "I have more to teach you," Father said. "You can do so much more than just that, with time."

Abigail looked at her father but said nothing.

"You won't tell your mother or Evelyn about this," Father said sternly. "This is our secret. Once you are older, you will appreciate these gifts."

Abigail's mother, Katherine, knelt in her garden, digging into the soil with a trowel. The Barrett family garden occupied a plot just outside of their home in the countryside, which was itself bordered by a low stone wall. Beyond, a cobbled road ran toward the village. The home was some decades old, but many of the family heirlooms and several pieces of furniture had been passed down to Arthur over several generations.

"Mother, what is in the woods across the river? Father said to never venture there." Abigail stood nearby, watching as her mother planted seeds that would grow into vegetables to set the family's dinner table during the coming summer. Abigail held several seedling packets, which she passed to her mother as the woman gestured for them.

"Oh, no one from the village goes there, that's why. A young girl went missing in those woods a while back. And some people before as well. The constable says it's a treacherous place, with sinkholes and the like."

Katherine stood up and brushed dirt from her apron. She looked down at her younger daughter; Abigail was short and slight, with wavy, light blonde hair and large, expressive brown eyes. She bore no close resemblance to either herself, her husband, or to her older sister Evelyn. "Just be a good girl and do as your father says," Katherine said brusquely. "You don't want to get into any trouble once school lets out."

Abigail followed her mother from the garden into the kitchen, observing Katherine as she removed her gardening gloves and washed her hands with a bar of soap in the kitchen sink. There were several weeks left of school before the summer break, and a classmate, Rachel, had asked Abigail to come with her into the woods to do some exploring.

"You're just scared, admit it! Scared of the woods, like a baby," Rachel had said, sticking her tongue out.

"No, I'm not," Abigail retorted anxiously.

"Well, we can't be friends anymore." Rachel made a face and began to walk away after standing from her spot on the park bench next to Abigail. The village's sole schoolyard was not far away.

"Wait, Rachel, please! I'll go. I want to see the woods too, but my father might find out. He told me to stay away."

Rachel stopped in her tracks, turned around slowly, and then smiled. "No, he won't," she said, her eyes flashing mischievously. "We'll leave for the woods right after our classes. We can hide our bicycles in the bushes near the schoolhouse and then slip away once we're dismissed. Our dads will never find out, nor will anyone else."

The thought of entering those woods, even in the daylight, worried Abigail, but Rachel was one of her few friends. Abigail was at the top of their village's small grammar school, and was ostracized by many of the other pupils because of this. She could have even advanced several years to the upper school, but Abigail's parents had decided against it.

Abigail didn't mind; in fact, she preferred to stay where she was. Certain boys at the upper school had long spread rumors concerning Abigail's father. Arthur Barrett was employed as a journalist and writer, with his articles appearing in various newspapers and publications. Word had reached their village that Mr. Barrett had written for "possibly blasphemous" journals printed overseas, with his articles in either French or German instead of English.

Rachel reassured Abigail: "No one wants to go there, so something must be important about the place. We'll just cross the old bridge, take a look around, and then ride back home on our bikes. We'll have hours of light—it's almost summer, after all!"

Abigail said nothing, but gave a sullen nod.

"Let's get back before they miss us," Rachel chirped, as if distracting Abigail from further discussion. She pulled Abigail up from the bench and took off back toward the village school. Classes would resume after lunch, and final exams were coming up in a few weeks' time.

"Hide it here, under the arch." Rachel grimaced as she trudged through the mud and leaned her bicycle against the damp stone of the long bridge that connected the village to the secluded woodlands beyond it. Abigail followed, wheeling her bicycle to the hiding place and propping it near Rachel's. This done, she turned to Rachel, as if awaiting instruction.

Rachel took a sack from her bike's iron basket and opened it to show Abigail the wax paper-wrapped sandwiches inside. "I nabbed these from the school canteen right before we left," she said, handing a sandwich to Abigail. "I'm faster than I look, eh?"

Abigail unwrapped a sandwich and took a bite.

Rachel had already gobbled hers down and was speeding up the river's embankment toward the bridge above. The old stone bridge was not well maintained, but it was solidly built. It had been here for as long as Abigail could remember, and for many years before that.

Unbeknownst to the girls or indeed to any of the villagers, the forest had once been home to a small settlement of shepherds and goat herders. The community had since been abandoned for reasons unknown.

Having caught up with her friend, Abigail peered across to the head of the bridge. It was a warm, cloudy day, the first of summer. Abigail wouldn't be noticed missing until hours from now when Mother would call her for the family dinner.

The forest appeared vast, almost endless, a thick canopy of deciduous trees and rolling hills stretching as far as they could see. Near the end of the bridge was a narrow, partially submerged path leading away into the forest.

"This way," Rachel said, following the path.

Abigail hurried behind her.

The two girls wandered for some time, the bramble undergrowth soon giving way to scores of broad oak trees, their low branches tangled together. The oaks' exposed roots intertwined over the barely visible pathway, slowing the girls' progress. Rachel climbed the raised roots in front of her as she advanced, appearing determined to penetrate to the heart of the woods itself.

After a long while, Abigail stopped. "This is just a deserted place, Rachel. Nothing is here." She wavered briefly and then said, "My mother told me a girl from the village was never found after coming into these woods by herself."

Rachel paused on the path before turning. "She was my cousin, Mary." She showed no emotion as she spoke.

Abigail looked at Rachel in surprise, waiting for her to continue.

"You wouldn't know her—she went to the upper school. It happened when we were quite young. I just wanted to see where it all took place. She'll never be found now."

Abigail's face fell, and she stepped forward to lay a hand on her friend's shoulder. "Rachel, I'm sorry. I only thought you wanted to come here as a dare, for some excitement. I didn't know this was personal for you."

Rachel sat down on the moss-covered roots of a towering oak, a tree that had perhaps seen the previous millennium as a sapling. She looked about the depths of the woods, surveying the maze of trees that stretched in all directions around her.

"You're right," she said after a long moment, her voice strangely quiet, "we should go back. I'm not sure what I wanted to find here, but now I've seen it."

Forcing a smile, Rachel stood and began tracing the path in front of her. Abigail watched her for a moment and made as if to follow, when something caught her eye in the hollow beneath the sprawling oak where Rachel had been seated.

The cavity at the base of the oak contained something. Abigail squinted in the shade, but the hollow was deep and dark, defying the late afternoon sunlight. She approached, crouching beside the roots, and then reached into the oak's dank cavity. It was no good—her arm wasn't long enough. Sighing, Abigail sat back against the oak's roots.

"Rachel, there's something here."

When no response came, Abigail rose, glancing around. She peered down the path Rachel had taken. Nothing.

Pleading under her breath, Abigail took off after her friend. She followed the obscured path for what felt like hours, finally stumbling into a natural formation almost entirely concealed by hanging moss and overgrowth. The formation had an entrance like that of a small cave.

Why didn't we see this the first time through? Abigail thought to herself. *Rachel might be playing a trick on me. Oh, I hope not. There might not even be a Cousin Mary.*

She stepped off the path among the trees and came to the formation's entrance, staring into its dim passageway. The distant sounds of dripping water echoed from somewhere deep inside, and the air within felt cool after the warm summer breeze of the woods. Abigail decided this was a place from which someone might pull a joke on her, so she went in.

The smooth stone passage ended in a woodland grotto, open to the sky above, overgrown, but clearly once used for some purpose. At the center of the grotto was a strange statue. No one else was there.

I hope Rachel didn't fall into one of those crevices Mother warned me about, Abigail thought.

The stone sculpture was very detailed. The figure stood on a pedestal, which was clearly delved from the same quarry as the statue itself. A representation of a bearded, hair-covered man with spiral horns and hooved goat legs, the figure held a set of pipes. Recalling Father's books, Abigail recognized the statue as a Roman faun from classical antiquity.

Has this statue been here since that time? Abigail wondered. *A work of art should be in a museum in London, not out in the woods where no one can see it.*

As she studied the faun's finely wrought face, something moved in the corner of her eye. The wind awoke, the branches of the sturdy elms and green shrubs of the grotto swaying, the clouds above swelling overcast and perilous as they traveled swiftly overhead. The statue extended its arms and placed the set of pipes to its lips. As Abigail staggered back, it began to play a haunting melody.

The song of the pipes drowned out the ominous rumbling of the gathering storm above, its music fixing Abigail in place. Thunder cracked and the winds whipped around her as the eerie yet seductive song swelled to a crescendo. Abigail tore her eyes away, spying something at the grotto's end—an unmoving Rachel spread out on a stone stab, lightning bursting in the sky above her.

Held fast by the pipes' song, Abigail walked to the altar of sacrifice and took in hand the ceremonial blade which rested at the base of the slab. Her wide, staring eyes looked down at the motionless form of Rachel—she was laid on her back, exposed and vulnerable. Tears swelling in her eyes, Abigail felt herself raise the ancient dagger over her head . . .

Evelyn opened her eyes sleepily and looked across at her sister's bed, upon which someone was resting. The curtained window was open, the moonlight shining in from the otherwise lightless country night. Abigail was facing her sister, a blanket draped over her, fast asleep.

Springing from her bed, Evelyn pulled the blanket from Abigail, tossing it to the bedroom floor. Her sister stirred, rolling over from her pillow to look up at Evelyn, still half-asleep.

"Where have you been?" Evelyn hissed angrily. "Mother and Father drove to the village and told the constable you never came home after school. There are men out looking for you at this moment."

Abigail sat up and rubbed her eyes without saying anything, her legs dangling over the side of the bed. In the dim light of the bedroom, Evelyn could see Abigail was still wearing her school dress, which was badly torn and soiled.

"Where am I?" Abigail finally said, her voice barely a whisper.

"You're at home, in our bedroom," replied Evelyn, frowning. "What in God's name happened to you?"

Abigail looked up at Evelyn for the first time and said, "I don't know." Evelyn turned on the nightstand lamp and saw Abigail's shoes lying at the foot of the bed, covered in mud. There was a trail of dirt from the bedroom window to where Abigail had slept.

The sisters heard a door creak open in the house and then hurried footsteps toward the hallway outside of their room. The bedroom door was flung open without warning.

"Abigail!" Katherine exclaimed, running toward the bed and hugging her daughter tightly. "I'm so glad you're safe! We'll let Constable Jarvis know that we've found you." She pushed Abigail away and held her at arm's distance, inspecting her daughter's face and clothes. "But the constable said your friend Rachel is missing as well. Where is she?"

Abigail gazed sluggishly at her mother and then her sister, as if confused by the question. "I can't remember," she said in a dead tone. "I don't even remember how I came home."

Father was now standing in the doorway dressed in his pajamas and slippers, his robe tied at the waist.

"Enough of this. Abigail, go back to sleep once your mother dresses you in your bedclothes." Father shut the bedroom window abruptly, making sure the window latch was locked in place. "I will call on the constable first thing in the morning. The search party can't be reached tonight —not unless I go looking for them myself." With that, he turned and marched from the room.

Katherine began to remove Abigail's dress, and Evelyn took some of her sister's nightclothes out of a drawer. Katherine paused as she lifted the torn dress Abigail was wearing over her daughter's head. She didn't say anything but pulled Abigail's bare arm toward the nightstand's lamp.

There were faint claw marks along her daughter's forearm, as if left by some large animal.

"Constable Jarvis discovered your bicycle next to Rachel's under a bridge today. The same bridge to the woods your father and I warned you not to enter." Katherine was somber as she relayed the news to Abigail. "This means you could be implicated in a crime if Rachel isn't found, even as a young girl."

Abigail positioned herself on a stool in the kitchen, listening to her mother intently. Abigail looked out the kitchen window and saw Evelyn working in the family garden. *Where is Father?* she thought.

She met her mother's eyes. "How, Mother? Rachel and I are friends—I loved her dearly."

"The constable's men will continue to search for Rachel, but it was explained to me there is the possibility of a criminal case if any more evidence against you is found. I will pray for both of us."

Katherine studied Abigail. She knew her young daughter couldn't have anything to do with Rachel's disappearance. Yes, her selective amnesia was disconcerting, but her condition, real or feigned, didn't mean she had actually harmed her friend.

"You can't recall how your bike ended up under the bridge? You were riding home from school, you stopped by the side of the road with Rachel, and then the next thing you remember is waking up in your bedroom at night?"

"Yes, Mother, that's all I remember. Now may I please go outside with Evelyn?" Abigail dropped from the stool and stood near the kitchen table, waiting to be dismissed.

"Go. But dinner will be ready in a few hours—once your father returns. The constable will want to speak with you again in a couple of days when the search is concluded." Katherine watched her daughter open the kitchen's side door and join her sister in the garden. There were already insinuations being made in the village about this apparent tragedy, with some of the villagers singling out Abigail as the culprit.

"You're a witch!" One of the boys threw a stone at Abigail, but it missed her, striking the tree behind instead. "And you killed Rachel!" Several older boys with handfuls of stones had cornered Abigail outside the schoolyard against a shady tree. Abigail moved to walk past them, but they blocked her exit.

"I'm telling Mrs. Thorpe!" Abigail cried out. She became very frightened as the three boys glared down at her and, despite herself, she began to cry. One of the boys turned and swore under his breath. Mrs. Thorpe was walking toward them at a brisk pace, her face as fearsome as ever. "It's that old bag, Mrs. Thorpe. Just walk away, don't look at her," he commanded.

Quickly, the boys slipped behind the tree where Abigail was cornered and then away from the school grounds.

"Abigail, are you all right?" Mrs. Thorpe crouched down beside her. "Do you know those boys' names? What class are they in?"

"No, but . . ." Abigail hesitated. This wasn't the first such incident. Most of the children at school had coolly ignored Abigail after Rachel disappeared, their parents telling them Abigail may have been to blame after word circulated through the village. Now, with yet another reason to resent her, their coldness was apparently turning to outright hostility. The last thing Abigail wanted was more trouble.

"No," she corrected herself, "I don't know who they are. They're in another class, but I'm not sure which one. I didn't get a good look at them as it happened so fast."

Mrs. Thorpe frowned, but decided not to push the matter. She moved to calm Abigail and said, "Just come back to the yard. You need to collect your things before heading home. You must let me know if something like this happens again."

Abigail watched as Mrs. Thorpe walked back to gather the other children in the schoolyard and lead them back inside. She reached down and picked up the stone that had nearly struck her from the foot of the tree. Red-faced from crying, Abigail squeezed tightly, then released her hand. The small grey toad croaked, and Abigail placed it into her dress pocket before walking back to the village school.

Abigail pressed her ear against her parent's bedroom door. The hallway was dark—she was supposed to be asleep.

Mother and Father had been arguing, so she'd crept down the hall to find out if they were discussing anything that might involve her. Evelyn was still deep in slumber, oblivious to her parents' raised voices.

"I've never felt right about Abigail. You know that, Arthur. Even my pregnancy with her was quite . . . difficult."

There was a pause.

"There were terrible nightmares up until her birth. You must remember how it was. I vowed I would never have another child after Abigail."

"Yes, but the doctor said nothing was wrong with you, at least not physically," Arthur replied. "He said it was all depression from a second pregnancy so soon after your first."

Abigail peered through the keyhole and caught a glimpse of her father trying to pull her mother close, only for her to move to the other side of their bed, glancing away from him.

"But here is the good news I promised you," her father continued, undeterred, "I've accepted an editorial position with *The Daily Sentinel*, the paper I told you about when we first considered moving away from Wiltshire. Relocating overseas will require applying for family passports, visas, and eventually new citizenship once we're settled in."

Katherine turned to face him again, and he smiled at her hopefully. "Arthur, I couldn't be more happy," she said, smiling weakly. "We need a fresh start after all of this. Even our friends no longer see us. We're not welcome here anymore."

She embraced her husband, and they sat down on the bed, Katherine resting her head on Arthur's shoulder.

"This is a permanent move; we'll be far away from Wiltshire," Arthur said, caressing Katherine's hair. "A new life in a new country. I'll be in the study for a while to go over some of the details. Try to get some sleep; I'll join you soon."

Abigail backed away as if struck and quickly dodged down the hallway, silently slipping into her bedroom and leaping into bed. A moment later, Arthur's head appeared in the bedroom doorway. He glanced at each bed in turn and, apparently satisfied, continued on toward his study.

He sat at his writing desk and reviewed the family's travel documents, considering how taking Abigail away from Wiltshire had changed the plans he had for her. Abigail would still one day reach her full potential under his tutelage as an Ovate. Too many of the villagers and local authorities had begun to suspect the truth—or at least part of it, including Katherine.

Arthur stood and selected a black leather-bound volume from among the many books lining the shelves of his study. The weighty tome was centuries old, with a golden sickle on its spine.

Returning to his desk, Arthur began to quietly read aloud, murmuring in a strange language. The wind outside the study's bay window stirred, the sudden rush of night air rattling the aged glass of its windowpanes.

Katherine lay on her bed half-asleep, breathing lightly. She reflected on the move from Wiltshire. Life in a new country, her husband with a new position, and a fresh start away from the enmity and social isolation that had plagued their family these last months.

Abigail must have gone into those woods, she thought, but could she really be the cause of Rachel's disappearance? Shortly before she realized she was pregnant with Abigail, and then throughout the term of her pregnancy, Katherine had suffered from a recurrent nightmare: a grove in the woods at twilight, a stone stab, and shadowy forms surrounding her.

Each time, the nightmare would play out in the same manner. Barefoot and in a sheer white gown, she would lie on the stone slab. A man (or was it a man?) appeared from among the dark forms and stood before her. She would awaken just as the man had knelt over her, reaching out with a clawed hand . . .

The first time the nightmare came upon her, she'd awoken the next morning with odd scratches on her arms and legs, but the marks had quickly faded. Afterward, she'd begun to feel a visceral craving for raw meat and organs from the butcher's, the purchases of which she hid from Arthur. Sharp pains, as if she were being kicked by some hooved animal inside her, persisted through the pregnancy, even though the doctor could find nothing wrong.

Katherine lay on her back, touching her stomach as she recalled her fear the unborn child would suffer a deformity or even be monstrous once delivered. But Abigail had been perfectly healthy as a baby—beautiful, even.

Yet there was always the lingering suspicion that something was wrong with Abigail. The moments when Katherine would catch her daughter studying her while they worked together in the garden or in the kitchen, a puzzling expression on her face. Abigail's frequent nighttime walks alone these last few years, and the sometimes-fitful sleeps she endured, waking Katherine in the middle of the night to find her daughter wide-eyed and terrified. Could Abigail, this lovely young girl, truly be a murderess?

Abigail was asleep, tucked up warmly in her bed. Outside her bedroom window, amid the moaning winds, the cloaked figure of a tall man stood in silence. The outline of stag's antlers protruded sharply from the tall man's head as he stared in through the window at Abigail. Abigail continued to sleep, oblivious to the man's presence.

Abigail peered around at Father's new study, which had been left open and unlocked. She held an oakwood cane across her lap, the length of which she examined, running her hand over its burnished shaft. The cane wore a silver metal handle in the shape of a ram's head with horns. She could hear her mother, who'd just been on the telephone, sobbing in the nearby living room.

The crying stopped. A moment later, Katherine walked into the study. Abigail quickly hid her father's cane under the writing desk.

"We will likely have to move to a rented home soon, Abigail," Katherine said, her eyes almost bloodshot. "I won't be able to keep up with the mortgage now that your father is gone. I'm sorry. I wanted better for you and your sister."

She let herself fall in front of Abigail's chair and hugged her child close, tears leaking down her cheeks. Finally, she straightened, sniffed, and dabbed at her eyes. "It's getting late. Go upstairs and get some rest. Evelyn is already asleep. The doctor gave me enough sedatives for her to last the next month."

Abigail slipped from the plush chair and stood in front of her mother, giving her a faint smile, as if to assent. Her mother slipped past her, and Abigail heard the bathroom door down the hallway shut, followed by sounds of incessant crying.

Out the study's window, the spacious yard stretched behind the house, obscured from their neighbors by rows of oak trees on either side. Mother had found Father hanging from a branch by a knotted rope among the copse of oaks at the yard's far end. The police had removed Father's body from the tree before Abigail and Evelyn had arrived home from school.

The night before, Father had called Abigail to his study in the family's new home, coming first to her room where she'd been reading alone. Father had seemed very distraught, his eyes wide with fear, his face pallid and grieved.

She'd followed him to his study, noting the heavy curtains of its picture window were drawn, blocking the panoramic view of the back garden. A jumbled pile of books lay on Father's desk, a black book with a gold sickle on its spine being the most prominent. It was as if the books had been torn from the study's shelves in a panic and then searched through, one after the other.

Arthur took Abigail by both arms. "Abigail, I'm not sure how to tell you this, but I must. You have a very special gift. Not one received from me, but from your real father." His breath came in ragged gasps, but he composed himself enough to continue: "There are sacraments of evil as well as of good in all of us, but how we choose to use these graces determines our fates. There are also places where shadows and the dwellers of twilight reach out to touch this world, if only imperceptibly. I started you on a path that may lead to a world of shadows, but—for your own sake—choose a different one once I am gone."

Holding a trembling hand to Abigail's cheek, Arthur kissed her goodnight. Finally, he led her to the study's door and then locked himself inside. Abigail returned to her bedroom to sleep.

Now, she rose from the writing desk and unlatched the study's back door. She walked to the sheltered copse where Arthur had hanged himself by the neck. There, among the oak trees, stood the Horned God. He embraced Abigail, and she embraced him in return.

The Thing in the Cupboard

T he cemetery was mostly empty in the early afternoon, one Tuesday. Jeremy and his grandfather stood alone in front of a newly installed headstone. Upon its surface, *MINGLE* was written in bold letters, with the name of Jeremy's deceased father underneath and the date of his passing—only a week ago.

Grandfather put a hand on Jeremy's shoulder. "Your father was a great salesman and networker, Jeremy. A man who could sell ice in the Arctic. We even buried him with his copy of *How to Win Friends and Influence People.*"

The boy turned to look up at his grandfather before he spoke. "I was wondering what book that was resting on his chest." Jeremy gazed at the granite tombstone and his father's freshly dug grave plot, feeling wistful but not quite sad.

Together, Jeremy and his grandfather walked back to the car Grandfather had taken to the funeral service that morning. Driving from out of town, Grandfather had picked up Jeremy from his foster home before heading out for the service. Jeremy was now an orphan; his mother had passed on a few years before his father when he'd been only ten years old.

Grandfather was a widower, as Jeremy's grandmother had died the previous year. She'd taken a fatal tumble down a flight of stairs in the family farmhouse, where she'd lived with Grandfather, some months after Jeremy's mother had been taken by cancer.

The car sped along the highway for some time, then took an exit onto a two-lane road, traveling away from the city limits. "You'll like living with me this summer, Jeremy," Grandfather said in an encouraging tone. "When your Aunt Sally and her new husband return from overseas, you'll move in with them. Sally said she couldn't bear the thought of burdening me with a young boy in my old age"—here, he shot Jeremy a wink—"and you're her only nephew, after all."

Jeremy glanced over at Grandfather and said in a flat voice, "Living in the country is going to be boring." He then looked out of the window again, watching the houses become sparser and the buildings give way to livestock behind painted fences, rows of hay bales, and fields of crops.

"What you call boring, I call peace and quiet," Grandfather quipped. "Our homestead is far from any neighbors, but there's plenty to do there. For example, help me with the chores."

Jeremy glanced back at Grandfather, this time saying nothing. *Living with this old geezer is going to be pure Hell*, he thought.

The surface of the single path road leading past a solitary rusted mailbox was rough and pitted with potholes. The ill-kept road provided a bumpy ride over a low hill and then on to the farmhouse, which rested among open fields that extended for miles around the house.

It was still afternoon when Jeremy and his grandfather finally pulled up in their sedan. Grandfather parked along the periphery of the house's semi-circular gravel driveway, and Jeremy climbed out. He shut the car door and surveyed the land around him, a hand shielding his eyes from the bright sun which hung in a nearly cloudless sky. Past the empty fields were patches of leafy trees dotting the landscape, rolling green hills stretching into the distance, and a few decrepit buildings nearby, which may have originally been part of the farm's operation.

The whitewashed farmhouse itself was at least a century old but was well-maintained, at least compared to the other buildings, which were remarkable for their peeling wood siding and boarded windows. There were two floors to the farmhouse and, above, a peaked red roof. Even in the crisp daylight, though, the antiquated structure seemed strange and frightening, as if the house were somehow being held in the past even as the world around it continued.

"I have your suitcase, Jeremy. You must like to travel light. Let's go inside and get something to eat." Grandfather walked up the steps to the farmhouse's front door, passing two varnished rocking chairs on the porch. The swinging door opened and then closed behind him.

Grandfather placed down a plate piled with food and then sat across from Jeremy at the kitchen table. He began eating, looking across at Jeremy as he did so.

"Jeremy, you're not eating," Grandfather said, his statement more an order than an observation.

Jeremy stared down at his plate and tried to identify the greyish mash heaped on it. "What is this?"

"Why, they're leftovers," Grandfather answered, shoveling another mouthful of mash onto his fork.

"And what were they before they were leftovers?" Jeremy inquired, almost worried at this point.

"Well, Jeremy, they were leftovers-to-be," Grandfather said matter-of-factly. He continued eating, practically wolfing down his meal.

Jeremy pushed the plate away and said, "I'm not hungry right now. You can eat mine."

Grandfather shrugged and said, "Suit yourself." He reached across the table and put Jeremy's plate next to his own nearly empty one.

"I'm going upstairs to unpack and lie down for a bit. I'll be back downstairs in a few hours." Jeremy got up from the table and started to take the creaking stairway up to the bedroom floor, heading toward the room Grandfather had designated as his earlier in the day.

As he reached the top of the staircase, Jeremy looked down into the kitchen below him. Grandfather locked eyes with Jeremy and grinned, the many creases on his face deepening as he did so. He heaped on yet more mash, shoveling it down with renewed vigor.

Jeremy's room was small and cramped; it had probably been a guest room at one time, or maybe even his mother's room. There was no furniture other than a simple bed and a squat dresser for some clothes, which was empty. Jeremy looked out the second-floor window and saw Grandfather ambling across a field to one of the old buildings near the farmhouse, a tin bucket in his hand.

The old man opened a side door and then disappeared inside the dilapidated building, closing the door behind him. The windows of the single-story structure were entirely boarded up, so Grandfather's activities were now inscrutable.

Jeremy scanned the area around the farmhouse visible from his window. There was a stone well with a moldering bucket dangling from a rope and rusted pulley not far from the front porch. It sat by itself in the open space near the fields, probably a relic from the farmhouse's early days. There was running water in the house's kitchen and bathroom, so the old well was likely dry now.

Feeling a sudden pang of hunger, Jeremy placed a hand on his stomach as it grumbled audibly. He thought hopefully to himself, *there must be something to eat other than that weird goop.*

He looked out the window again. Grandfather didn't appear to be coming back to the house—he must still be in that rickety building doing whatever. Jeremy decided to search the kitchen for anything remotely edible.

The floorboards and stairs groaned as Jeremy hurried into the deserted kitchen and opened its bulky refrigerator, an appliance from a bygone era. Alongside it was a large wooden cupboard built into the kitchen wall.

He inspected the packed shelves, finding only sealed plastic containers full of the grey mush, a jar of dill pickles, and one stick of butter in a tray. *How does Grandpa live on this stuff? We're going to have to go grocery shopping tomorrow,* Jeremy decided.

Bringing the jar of pickles to the kitchen table, he removed its lid with some effort and speared one with a fork, lifting it to munch hungrily on one end.

From behind, Jeremy heard a slow creaking sound coming from the hanging cupboard above the kitchen countertop. He turned his head while still facing the table and, out the corner of his eye, saw the cupboard's door open.

Still holding the impaled pickle, Jeremy turned and stood in front of the open cupboard. The interior was quite dark and surprisingly deep, extending farther back into the kitchen walls than its contours would suggest.

A shape shifted around in the shadows, huddling at the back. The thing breathed, the sound nasal and rasping. "You must kill your grandfather, Jeremy," the creature spat in a sinister tone. "He is planning on harming you tonight. You must push him down the well outside once you have the chance."

Wide-eyed, Jeremy put a hand over his mouth and peered into the depths of the cupboard, trying to make out the creature. It seemed to be a hairless rodent of some sort, about the size of a large cat. It was too dark to see more than that.

Jeremy stepped forward, more curious than afraid.

"Stop that! Don't look at me," the creature hissed. "You must stay back."

Jeremy froze and then stepped back toward the kitchen table, putting his fork down. "What are you?" he said cautiously.

"I am the rightful owner of this house. I can say no more than that," the creature pronounced, its voice grating. "Now, close the cupboard door and do not say a word to your grandfather about me. You ignore my warning at your peril."

Not knowing what else to do, Jeremy shut the cupboard door and went back upstairs to sit on his bed. "Was that real?" Jeremy asked himself. "It had to be. There is something genuinely off about this place and about Grandfather. Maybe that horrible thing is telling the truth."

Jumping up from the bed, Jeremy peered once more out the window. He saw Grandfather walking back from the decrepit building, a bucket full of something hanging around his knee. The sun was beginning to set, its red glow lighting up the landscape around the farm.

Jeremy heard the farmhouse's front door creak open and the sound of a heavy bucket being put down somewhere in the house. "Jeremy!" came his grandfather's voice. "Come downstairs and join me on the porch. Let's watch the sunset together before it gets too late."

The moon's white light entered through the curtainless window, allowing Jeremy to make out the outline of the dresser pushed up against the bedroom door. He lay very still on his bare mattress, waiting for Grandfather.

After removing his clothes from its drawers, Jeremy had slowly pulled and pushed the weighty dresser to the door. He was almost certain he hadn't made much noise—at least, not enough to alert Grandfather. Jeremy had then sat on the floor in the darkened room and knotted his bedsheets into a rope. This, in turn, was tied between the bars of the bed frame's brass headboard and could be thrown over the ledge of the window if Jeremy needed to escape.

The light fixture on the ceiling above held no bulbs, its sockets empty. Jeremy felt the handy, club-like flashlight protruding from his pants pocket, the last present his father had given him before leaving this world so suddenly.

Something Grandfather had said while the two sat on the farmhouse porch that evening had made Jeremy very afraid. He'd not been threatening or outwardly malicious —rather, it was that he'd not known something, and had reacted so strangely when corrected.

"Life in the country is so much better, Jeremy. Why, if your mother were with us, she would tell you the same. Gertrude loved growing up in this house." Grandfather rocked back and forth in his chair, a halcyon smile on his face. A warm evening breeze drifted over the porch, yet Jeremy felt a sudden chill.

Jeremy stopped rocking and looked at the old man quizzically. "Gertrude was grandma's name, Grandpa. Emma was my mother—your daughter. Are you all right?"

"Of course, I just forgot. I'm an old man, Jeremy." Grandfather had stopped smiling. He was staring at Jeremy as he rocked back and forth in his chair, as if assessing whether Jeremy had believed his excuse.

Was Grandfather some sort of imposter? Jeremy thought back to the bizarre creature and its warning, still not sure whether he'd really seen the thing. It had happened so fast. Normally, he'd have assumed Grandfather was telling the truth—he was an old man, after all—but something about his peculiar reaction told Jeremy otherwise.

Jeremy hadn't seen his grandfather for quite some time before his father's funeral that morning. In fact, the last time had been at Jeremy's grandmother's burial. The services had been held at a local church not far from the farmhouse.

There was a shuffling noise outside the bedroom door. Jeremy put both feet on the floor and reached for the knotted bedsheets nearby.

The bedroom doorknob twisted and rattled, the weight of the dresser preventing the door from opening. The door then shook as something slammed against it from outside, the dresser budging slightly from its spot. With enough force, Grandfather would soon get through.

Jeremy moved quickly, unlatching the bedroom window, and pushed its lower panel up to climb down the side of the farmhouse. He tested the bedsheet rope fastened to the bed's frame and then began to crawl over the sill.

The attack on the bedroom door was very loud now, and Jeremy heard the sound of splintering wood just as he disappeared over the window's ledge, gripping the taut bedsheets and dropping safely to the ground below.

He ran through the fields toward the boarded-up building Grandfather had entered earlier. He glanced back as he ran, finding Grandfather climbing down the bedsheet rope, his hunched body glinting in the moonlight.

Jeremy found the door to the battered barn-like structure unlocked and slipped inside. Very little moonlight entered through the gaps in the boards, sealed windows, and sagging roof. A dank, earthy smell permeated the place, but nothing blocked his way as he felt along the walls and then curled up in a tight corner. He had no idea what might be in there with him, but Jeremy was too scared to risk turning on his flashlight.

Grandfather called out into the night, "Jeremy, you can't escape from me. There's nowhere to run. There's nothing around here for miles, my boy." Jeremy realized that Grandfather's voice now sounded evil, just like the thing in the cupboard.

Something wriggled across the top of Jeremy's hand as it lay pressed in the dirt. He cautiously turned on his flashlight, fearing the worst—but it was just a few dozen earthworms burrowing into the earthen floor.

Jeremy arced the flashlight's beam across the length of the room and saw the entire space was teeming with thick, bloated earthworms—many thousands of them—writhing in the freshly turned up soil. Feeling a rising sickness, Jeremy abruptly turned off the flashlight. He could hear his grandfather approaching.

Something passed by outside, obstructing the moonlight filtering through the cracks in the wallboards. Grandfather was coming—he would soon reach the door to the barn.

Jeremy dashed toward a patch of the barn wall where the moonlight was glimmering through the gaps. He felt around desperately, finally finding it—a loose board. He pushed it aside and squeezed through the opening, stepping out into the warm night.

As Jeremy turned, his flashlight illuminated Grandfather's manic face. Crying out, Jeremy staggered back—his grandfather's eyes were inky pools of pitch-black: inhuman and otherworldly.

Swinging low, Jeremy struck Grandfather in the knee with this flashlight, bringing him down. Grandfather snarled, making halting attempts to stagger to his feet as Jeremy ran from him.

The second farm building further out loomed ahead. Jeremy shut off his flashlight, hoping it would stop Grandfather from finding him right away. This building was smaller than the barn, its sole window boarded, with a swinging door clattering in the breeze. Jeremy burst in, shutting the door behind him, and turned on his flashlight.

A circular glyph was chalked in dark red at the center of the plank floor. Nearby were framed pictures of Jeremy's mother, along with some of her personal items, which rested on a kind of crude altar outside of the circle. Placed at the foot of the altar was a book bound in crimson leather, an ornate symbol on its cover.

Jeremy opened the book. Its title was *On the Mysteries and Rites Related to the Resuscitation of Those Passed*, dated 1712. No author was given. Turning its pages, Jeremy was greeted by detailed, grotesque illustrations of horrid beings, utterly alien to this world.

Setting the book down, Jeremy searched the shed's tools for something he could use as a weapon, and found a solid metal rake. He directed his flashlight to the occult glyph on the floor and noticed its chalk circle had been broken somehow, smeared and now incomplete.

Jeremy shut the flashlight off and eased open the shed door, grasping the iron rake in both hands. He walked out into the nighttime fields, the full moon large overhead, and saw Grandfather's form in the distance. The old man appeared to be resting against the stone well near the farmhouse, apparently unaware that Jeremy had emerged from the shed. He limped stiffly around the well before beginning to lower its bucket into the depths of the shaft. The pulley squeaked to a halt, and Grandfather leaned over the well's edge, calling out in a strange tongue to something at the well's bottom.

Dropping the rake as he ran, Jeremy leaped out of the darkness, pushing Grandfather headfirst into the well. The old man made a terrible, piercing shriek as he plummeted down the long shaft, but no sound was heard once the figure vanished from Jeremy's sight. Even with a flashlight, the bottom of the well shaft wasn't visible—there was only darkness.

Jeremy stumbled back to the farmhouse, emotionally drained and almost numb. The figure of a man stood in the moonlight on the steps of the front porch, his features not yet visible. The man did not move; he seemed to be waiting for Jeremy.

Approaching cautiously, Jeremy pointed his flashlight into the figure's face. It was his grandfather.

The old man smiled at Jeremy, holding his arms wide to embrace him. Jeremy ran to him, and they hugged one another, neither saying a word.

"I hope Jeremy wasn't too much trouble," Aunt Sally said, placing her hand on Jeremy's head as she tousled his sandy hair.

Grandfather gave her a warm smile. "No, not all. Jeremy was very helpful around the farm. We even dug up the barn's dirt floor and filled it back in. That's quite a project for just one old man and a boy."

"I'm glad he was able to help you out, Dad," Aunt Sally said, "especially now you're all alone out here. Jeremy will be starting school again soon, but we'll be back to you see at Christmas."

Aunt Sally gave her father a final hug before leading Jeremy to her car. Her husband, who was waiting behind the wheel in the driver's seat, gave Grandfather an awkward wave.

As Jeremy opened the car's back door, he turned to look at Grandfather, who remained standing on the steps of the farmhouse porch. The old man nodded to him but said nothing, only watching as the car pulled away.

Grandfather walked back inside the farmhouse, took a well-worn bowl from the kitchen's cupboard, and placed it on the table. He opened the refrigerator and removed several pieces of raw meat from a thin, transparent wrap, putting them into the bowl.

Grumbling something under his breath, he opened the low door to the farmhouse's cellar. He set the bowl of morsels at the top of the stairs and then stepped back, watching closely.

A small, clawed hand, withered and covered in loose grey skin, reached out from the lightless space. The hand snatched the scraps from the bowl and then disappeared, receding back into darkness.

The Lady Cornwall

I was born to be a seaman, and it's all I've ever endeavored to be. From my youth and then into the first days of a looming dotage, my years were spent sailing the oceans of the world, living a life those who seek comfort and safety would never dare consider. Why should I have settled for a life unlived, never testing my true worth? Every man is born as many men, but he dies as just one.

But where shall I start this odd and unusual tale, this unbelievable encounter with things unknown and unexplainable? At the beginning, of course, where all good stories start.

I was hired as a crew member onto *The Invictus*, a newly constructed seaworthy vessel bound for trade waters charted by many previous crews and cartographers. The ship's captain, one Captain John Miles, told the new recruits he needed men who were not just brave but fearless, men who could drink death like fine wine if the occasion called for it.

Captain Miles promised the crew pay well above grade as well as a substantial bonus once we secured our cargo at the predestined unloading port on the other side of the ocean. What our cargo was, however, Captain Miles did not say, but the hint of danger was present, commensurate with our excellent salary.

The Invictus left our northern port of call along the balmy coast and sailed out into the vast ocean, passing between continents, fading from the sights of civilized men and their predilections. Our ship traveled for days without incident, making good time along our course. The crew was at ease and confident, the waters calm and accommodating.

But on the seventh day, the weather changed drastically —and not for the better. A terrible tempest seized upon us, forcing us off course and into waters absent on any map. The events that would follow this dreadful storm are so incredible, so beyond belief, that I would surely forgive you if you gave them no credence.

At first, the early evening was mild—the softly glowing sky was as clear as it had been at noontime that day. We sailed over tranquil waters as the sun began to set on the horizon, suffusing the top decks of our ship with a soothing warmth. We allowed ourselves to believe a long summer at sea lay ahead.

Then, though, dark clouds began to gather overhead. It was as if a thick, woolly canopy had been drawn over our vessel, covering the entirety of the sky. We heard thunder, and then saw flashes of lightning on the horizon. A squall on the open waters unlike any of us had ever seen would soon come upon us.

The frothing waves around our ship began to heave, and heavy rain started to fall. We tried to maintain control— Gods, we tried—but we rode the crashing waves and fierce winds like a bucking horse, wild and untamed.

The storm winds lashing around him, Captain Miles shouted above the roaring din of the rising typhoon: "Bring down the sails or they'll be torn from the masts! Quickly, men, now!"

The crew acted with utmost speed, but the high winds were far too vicious. Ocean water rushed over the decks, striking an unlucky crewman and sweeping him overboard —he was gone before any of us could even reach the rail, lost to the swirling abyss. Our once-mighty ship was but a mote in the whirlwind, dancing about the treacherous waters.

Without warning, an enormous cresting tidal wave appeared above the ship and seemed as if it would drag *The Invictus* down into a watery grave—but, instead, we were tossed away by the storm winds. The gigantic wave crashed behind the ship's stern, spraying its decks with Neptune's bile.

The force of it flung our ship from the roughest waters near the center of the tempest into considerably less turbulent seas. We glided through without sails—as the captain warned, they'd been torn away almost entirely.

The storm roiled around us for some time until it stealthily rolled back, almost as quickly as it had come. It was night, the skies above clear again, full of sparkling stars and constellations for which no charts existed.

The crew worked under the light of lanterns and hung new sails onto the square-rigged masts of our full-rigged ship. The winds were dead now, eerily still after their violent exhibition only a few hours afore.

By morning, the ocean winds had picked up again, and we sailed once more over calm waters. The crew was beginning to panic as the ship's navigator could set no course—our nautical maps were useless in these strange, uncharted waters.

The captain attempted to reassure the crew, claiming our situation was only temporary, that we would soon find our way back to land and then a friendly port. The steward checked our supplies and informed us we could not be lost for long as our surplus was limited, allowing for a few months at most.

For several days and several nights, we sailed almost blind, looking for familiar star patterns or signs of land on the horizon. But on the third night, our barrelman cried out to us, having spotted a vessel not unlike our own from the crow's nest.

The ship was a three-masted barque, hanging stationary in the distance. The captain examined the possibly derelict ship through his looking glass, the large moon overhead bathing the craft in a spectral blue light.

The translucent thing bopped on the waters, swaying as the waves dashed against its hull. Its sails were down, its decks empty of crewmen or any signs of life at all. The cold white barque seemed like a rare jewel on the dark waters of the unfamiliar sea, enticing us toward it.

The captain gave the order to board, reasoning that we locate some clue as to our whereabouts on its premises. We pulled in our ship's sails and sat still on the water. The captain, first mate, myself, and several other crewmen formed the boarding party and stood near the rail, peering over at the nearing hulk.

The crew lowered one of the ship's two gigs down the side of our vessel, and the six of us oared to our destination. A chill spread over me as our gig came to rest near the barque's starboard side. Peering up at the silent ship, I thought it a floating tomb, the resting place of dead men lost at sea.

We slowly rowed along the starboard side, examining the ship's hull with our glowing lanterns. Below the ship's bow was the carved figurehead of a beautiful woman in flowing white robes, her back arched toward the sea. The name *The Lady Cornwall* was etched in gold lettering along the side of the ship's upper hull, framing the figurehead's bare feet.

We moored against the hull and scaled the shrouds hanging loosely along its starboard side. The deck from the ship's fore to its aft was entirely empty, but a door to the decks below was open and lightless, impenetrable in the dark of night.

The captain raised his lantern before him and motioned for us to follow. We climbed slowly down the flight of stairs into the belly of the ship, finding a cabin near the stairwell whose door had also been left wide open.

It was spacious, and appeared to have belonged to the ship's captain. A porcelain cup set on its saucer was on the table, filled with brewed coffee, still warm to the touch. A map of the waters near our original port of departure lay next to it, folded open, with a ship's nautical compass and a sextant nearby.

We ventured on, peering into the other cabins, all of which showed signs of recent occupation: The crew's sleeping quarters had recently slept-in bunks, tables with playing cards laid out, as well as cooling cups of coffee and edible food on plates. The ship's galley was not bare, but instead was stocked with fresh foodstuffs. It was as if the crew had stood up amid their daily activities and walked as one out into the ocean, vanishing forever.

After a thorough search of the ship, we found nothing to inform us of our plight. The mystery of why the ship's crew had disappeared so suddenly, apparently near our departure port, felt like an omen of what would eventually befall our own ship. We resolved to find our way back to dry land and survive this test of our strength and will, to live to tell the tale I am telling you now.

First commandeering the choicest supplies for our crewmen, we unmoored our gig from *The Lady Cornwall* and rowed the small patch of ocean back to *The Invictus*. After boarding our ship, we bedded down to sleep for the remainder of the night, and hoped favorable winds would return to us in the morning. The quartermaster would account for the enigmatic ship's excess stock the following day.

I was lying in my cot that night, unable to find sleep, when I heard sails being hoisted and the night watchman cry out, "The ship, she looks about to set sail! But there's no crew about her!"

We rushed from our cabins above decks and saw full sails billowing about the masts of *The Lady Cornwall*, swollen in the cool ocean wind. The ship tilted to one side and began to sail into the darkness, away from our ship and into waters we had not yet explored. No captain or crew could be seen on the ship's upper deck—I told myself the clouded dark of the dead of night must be to blame.

The unfurled sails of *The Invictus* impelled us forward, giving chase to *The Lady Cornwall*. We followed the ghost ship over the seas, pacing behind her for at least one hour's time. What we hoped to accomplish I cannot say, but we prayed *The Lady Cornwall* might lead us to our eventual rescue . . . and not, the good Lord forbid, our doom.

The distance between *The Invictus* and *The Lady Cornwall* grew as we sailed, until the ethereal ship was but an insignificant dot on the night sea. An uncanny fog had rolled out over the surface of the ocean, darkish green in hue, as if emanating from the ghost ship itself. It grew thick and eerie, roiling about us as we sailed into its midst, dim orbs floating within its saturnine depths.

The Lady Cornwall could no longer be seen. In fact, nothing was visible save the preternatural fog that enswathed *The Invictus* like a smothering tarpaulin. We sailed into what we knew might be oblivion—there was no other recourse.

A bright light appeared in the center of the fog, directly ahead of our ship's bow. We sailed forward, grasping at this single chance to possibly break through the fog and finally find land—and it grew, eclipsing the murky shades of fog and replacing them with a radiant yellow sheen. *The Invictus* cut through the wall of fog and emerged into cleansing daylight, a warm blue-green sea stretching out in every direction. The fog behind us was gone.

There was no sign of *The Lady Cornwall*. The captain took his spyglass and searched for a coast or an island where we might find safe harbor, anywhere that promised at least temporary succor. And yes, there was something: a mountainous island with a long shoreline, perhaps but a league away.

We came to rest in the littoral waters near a sandy beach unmarred by the intrusions of men. Our ship's two gigs made several trips back and forth until most of her crew was on land, the first we had seen since departing on this mad expedition.

The island was tropical, humid, and unfavorable to men such as ourselves. Great palmed trees spanned much of its interior, while the undergrowth near the beach was dense and brushed continually against us as we strode forth to explore.

A natural path through the jungle led up the side of a steep, sloping cliff nearby. We assembled on this plateau, which offered a bird's-eye view of the island's dense interior. The many spires of an unknown city were visible to us now, set deep within the lush confines of the island's primeval jungle.

The calls of feral animals echoed over our heads as we slashed away at the ripe vines that blocked our egress, laying a passageway through the jungle inland. The tangled bush was resistant to our cutlasses but not invulnerable and, by late in the day, we'd found the outskirts of the city.

We stood on the threshold of a vast stone metropolis, bizarre in its structures and antediluvian in its appearance —a city that seemed somehow to predate humanity itself given the size of its buildings, whose inhabitants surely would have to have been giants.

But the city was empty. Not a soul could be seen as we passed its towering monuments and walked its broad avenues, long since vacated. The sound of our footsteps on stone was all that could be heard.

An enormous eye set in relief above its columnated entranceway, massive stone steps carved from volcanic rock led to a temple dedicated to forgotten gods. The unblinking, cyclopean eye seemed to burn in its resting place, though it was as cold as any other stone.

The sun was beginning to set over the island's horizon, and Captain Miles ordered the crew to make camp under the temple's edifice. Campfires dotted the smooth floors under the temple's pillars like fireflies, and a tent was erected for the captain and his first mate.

A watchman was set at the temple steps, and the men fell into slumber. I was struck by the silence—it seemed as if the nighttime sounds of the tropical wilderness could not penetrate the enclosures of the stone city, which remained uncommonly still and quiet.

Then I heard it. At first, it was only a whisper in the wind, but the awful shrieking soon grew closer. There was not one, but many of them, coming in the darkness from the temple itself, from within the lightless corridors engraved with abominable depictions of obscene rites and rituals.

Bulbous, staring eyes in the dozens; masses of glistening, grotesque flesh; trails of caustic slime spawned from the ocean's primordial ooze. The shambling horrors were upon us with ferocious speed before we could arise, tossing the crew about like ragged dolls, feeding them into gaping maws with hook-suckered tentacles.

The men who survived the savage onslaught ran from the temple into the night-shrouded city, hearing the distant screams of Captain Miles and the first mate echoing behind them.

I, with those left of our expedition, unmoored our landed gig from the shores of the beach and pushed it out into the waters. We rowed furiously back to *The Invictus*, the monstrosities howling with bloodlust as they clambered through the jungle behind us.

Now with only a skeleton crew and no captain, we drifted into the sea around the island, cursing the ill fortune that had come upon us. Even if another island refuge were found, how did we know it wouldn't also be inhabited by monsters dredged from the depths of Hell itself?

We soon spied *The Lady Cornwall* in the moonlight, coasting within a league of our ship. Why the vessel had disappeared the first time and why it now returned to us, I may never know. The ghost ship sailed through the night, passing by our ship's port side, as if inviting *The Invictus* to follow her yet again.

In our fear and madness, we pursued with no apparent purpose. She sped forward, enlarging the gap between the two ships, racing ever faster into what would become a yawning void in the ocean.

Once again out on the open ocean with no land in sight, the waters beneath us began to churn. We found we had sailed into an immense vortex, our hapless ship turning in ever-dwindling circles toward the center. *The Invictus* was pulled under by the maelstrom, sinking into the trenches of the alien ocean, taking her drowning crew with her.

In the near darkness, my lungs filling with brine, I saw a vast underwater graveyard of ships stretched out below. Some were from past ages, while others were of a like I had never before witnessed. These strange ships seemed built of solid metal from stern to bow, with no observable masts or sails.

Where I am now, I can't quite say. Some may call this place Hell, while others might name it Purgatory. I now share this ghostly ship with men from many ages and nations; we sail the seas for all time, luring seamen to their deaths beneath the waves. This is my fate, to forever remain a crewman on *The Lady Cornwall*.

The Story Writes Itself

B rother Jacob labored alone in his scriptorium, hunched over an illuminated manuscript. The book's engraved cover would soon be inlaid with ivory and silver, the last step in its lengthy creation process. He stared down at the religious text's most recently completed page and felt the anticipation of this work reaching its fruition.

A detailed illustration of the Archangel Uriel peered back at him, guarding the entrance to Heaven. The hand-painted color picture was highlighted against the page's bold Latin script. Jacob thought it was quite a striking composition, even distracting the reader from the written words on the page.

The learned monk was growing older, his eyes weary, his demanding work schedule beginning to take its toll on his declining health. Soon, though, the sacred text would be in the hands of the monastery's abbot. The book was the product of a years-long effort by Brother Jacob—he'd toiled by himself for countless hours in solitude.

Coughing into his closed hand, Brother Jacob turned to the massive tome's last page. The vellum lay blank, waiting to be filled.

A quill set between his fingers, he drew the outline of the manuscript's final illustration—a depiction of the Archangel Michael slaying a demonic entity with his flaming sword. The archangel stood atop his foe's back; Jacob smiled—evil would always be defeated by the divine.

His pen moved quickly across the soft paper, his efficiency the result of his many years' hard-earned experience. Jacob thought the illustration and transcription of its accompanying words would take this night and then five nights more, ending this chapter of his life's hallowed calling.

The candle burning in the holder atop his raised writing bench flickered, as if disturbed. The already darkened room became momentarily more shadowed than before.

The monk stood from his scribe's stool, rubbing his eyes, and then stepped away from the bench. He carefully snuffed the flame of the melting candle with a tarnished brass douter and set his quill aside for the night.

He left his monk's cubicle, exiting into the adjoining hallway of the monastery. The sole source of light was now a wrought-iron lamp hanging from a wall hook at the distant end of the corridor.

A sudden draft swirled through the stone-lined hall. Brother Jacob paused—*What was that noise?* He turned to peer down the corridor. Darkness—nothing else besides.

The monastery hall was quiet and empty, his fellow brothers asleep in their cells. *I'm just tired*, Jacob thought. *It's time to lay on my cot and visit with my dreams. Where else can I find some peace from the abbot?*

He continued down the hallway toward the hanging lamp, the previously muted luminescence of its light now more prominent. A soft moan came from somewhere behind him.

The moan sounded very real, as if it were not merely the result of a gust of air wafting between the stones of the monastery's walls. Jacob turned again, this time noticing a dark shape forming in the shadows of the hallway's passage.

He strode on quickly, his weary legs carrying him toward the lamp and, beyond it, his cell. Harsh winds billowed through the hall and swirled about Jacob, as if from nowhere, the hem of his robe whipping under the force of the gale.

He turned once more into the face of the battering winds. A low growl emanated from somewhere at the passage's end, a whiff of sulfur reached him—and then a monstrous black figure began to rise from the bare stone floor. The entity spread wide its cloaked arms and enveloped the saintly monk, Brother Jacob plunging into its chthonic depths with a silent scream.

Brother Jerome eased open the metal lid of the hanging lamp, finding it spent from the night before. It was morning, and he was making his rounds through the monastery. The young monk continued down the hallway to the monastery's scriptorium, pausing in front of Brother Jacob's writing space.

The room was unoccupied, the monk nowhere to be found. An illuminated manuscript rested on the room's writing desk, open to the last page.

Jerome stood above the desk, frowning. The richly colored illustration on the open page appeared fresh, the ink vivid and dark—it showed a man, a monk, being dragged down to Hell by many horned devils. In the lower section of the illustration, the devils tortured the man, boiling him alive in a cauldron brimming with caustic oils.

Turning away from the blasphemous depiction, Brother Jerome wondered what could have possessed Brother Jacob to draw such a malevolent scene of cruel punishment.

Carter Smith was almost nodding off in his wingback chair when Ms. Mooney's sharp question brought him back around. He pulled himself up and once again focused his attention on the young woman. She'd been sent by a national newspaper to compose a human-interest story about Carter, albeit of little interest to him.

Had she noticed? Carter squirmed in his seat, watching the woman jot something into the hand-sized binder resting on her lap. If she had, she gave no indication. Instead, she looked up from her plush wingback on the far side of the room and gave Carter a tight smile.

Carter had only agreed to this morning's interrogation to please his long-time publisher, Bartleby & Bayne. Carter's recently published novel, *The Delgado Cipher*, was a bestseller, and thus a major win for his publishing house. The novel was being heralded in the press as Carter's best effort to date, and the attention had invited a flood of interview requests as well as the usual puff pieces in popular magazines.

Carter didn't mind the attention—in fact, he loved it—but he still hated interviews. He would feel weighed down by what he believed were insipid queries presented by someone unfamiliar with his writing. But this novice journalist's last question had been uncharacteristically insightful. Perhaps Ms. Mooney was an astute reader after all.

She looked up from her notepad, still wearing that tight smile, and cleared her throat. "*The Delgado Cipher* has been atop several bestseller lists for months now; it's arguably your greatest success. What do you think makes this book so special?"

She peered at him expectantly, going so far as to lean toward him. It seemed as if Carter's reply might be the angle she was seeking for *The Daily Sentinel*'s Sunday edition.

Carter became animated, partially to conceal that he was reciting one of his prepared answers and partially to wake himself up. "It's the air of mystery about the book, certainly; the genuine feeling of uncovering a hidden past for humanity. No one has quite addressed this subject matter the way I have in *The Delgado Cipher*." Carter leaned back, smiling brightly.

Ms. Mooney gave a curt nod, then said, "*The Delgado Cipher* is reputed to contain secret symbolism, even a code based on the names and numbers that appear in the novel. Do you believe the hype around this purported secret code has added to the book's popularity?" She seemed very serious, almost as if she were probing Carter to see if he would lie in response.

Carter chuckled dismissively and said, "My readers have conjured up a number of conspiracy theories around the book, but they are just that—theories. I'm sorry to say I'm not clever enough to weave some esoteric message into my writing. Of course, people can believe what they want."

This time, Ms. Mooney continued to write for several long minutes. Finally, she stood, closed the small black binder, and then reached to shake Carter's hand. "Thank you very much, Mr. Smith. It was a great interview. I'm really appreciative of your time today." She slipped her binder into her purse and gave Carter a broad smile.

Carter forced a genial smile in return and then led Ms. Mooney to the rear door of his secluded home. The two walked through a small, partially enclosed garden to the exterior of Carter's house, and Carter opened the garden's wrought-iron gate.

Ms. Mooney's compact car was parked against the curb on the other side of the garden's hedge. She waved briefly to Carter as she drove off, leaving him by himself on the empty drive.

Here is what Carter Smith had found jarring about the interview: not the final question about the "secret code" supposedly ensconced in his latest book, but the question immediately before concerning the lengthy period which had passed between this most recent novel and his previous one.

During the first half of the interview, Ms. Mooney had offered nothing but pat, mostly formulaic questions—his favorite author, what in the horror and dark fantasy genres influenced him as an adolescent, what he thought of his many fans, and so on—but then she'd said something piercing: "Mr. Smith, you've been a highly prolific writer for many years, publishing over two dozen novels, all of them with three-word, two-word, or even one-word titles. Yet, before *The Delgado Cipher*, there was a roughly three-year gap in which you published literally nothing." Ms. Mooney had paused before she spoke again. "If I may ask, what happened?"

It was true: Carter had suffered from severe writer's block for almost two years. Every day, he'd sat at his desktop computer for an hour at a time and then found something with which to distract himself.

Typing just a single sentence into a blank document file had quickly become a struggle. Long walks in the early evening after a squandered morning and afternoon failed to clear his head, and reading other authors became a waste of time. Nothing could inspire Carter to write even in short bursts.

At first, Carter told himself his writer's block was a consequence of entering early middle age; he no longer had either the enthusiasm for writing or the stamina he'd possessed as a younger man. He would sleep in later, take longer walks, eat healthier meals, and other remedies to make himself right again.

But Carter's listlessness and melancholy continued, day after day until months had passed, and then more than a year. Frustrated and worried his career as an author might be finished, Carter decided to take an extended vacation overseas. His hope was that this sabbatical would finally end his terrible paralysis and allow him to write again.

He resolved to visit the rural southwest of England; he'd spend the summer there and wouldn't leave until he believed himself cured. Carter had researched the region, and the pictures he had found on the Internet set his mind at ease. But what Carter discovered in the tiny village where he took his rest changed him and his writing in ways he had never anticipated.

Carter gave Ms. Mooney a slow, deliberate response, as if he were reliving the events of those years. "After *The Faithful* was published, the novel sat on the bestseller lists for several weeks and then fell off, with dwindling sales afterward. I decided I needed not only a break from writing but to reflect on where my life was going. My hiatus ended after a summer spent relaxing in a quaint English village named Avebury. Have you heard of it?"

"I'm sorry to say I haven't," Ms. Mooney replied, suddenly taking an interest.

"A beautiful place," Carter told her. "It's the epitome of what people mean when they use the word 'pastoral.' A community and a region steeped in ancient history.

"I spent a summer there, got some serious reading done in my rented house, and I was able to get back to productive writing before leaving the village.

"I wouldn't have been able to complete *The Delgado Cipher* without my summer reprieve. At present, I'm planning my next book, *The Possessed*. The tentatively scheduled publication date is later this year."

Ms. Mooney arched her eyebrows. "So, your readers can expect regular output now that you're back at writing?"

"Yes, quite certainly," Carter said cheerily. "Writing comes very easily to me again. It's almost as if the stories write themselves."

"You kept a straight face through the whole thing? I don't believe it." Jane threw back her head, the sound of her laughter rising above the noisy surroundings of the newsroom. She leaned against the edge of Sarah Mooney's desk in the open office area and grinned.

Sarah sat in her desk chair, shuffling through her handwritten notes from the interview she'd completed earlier in the day. She smirked without looking up and said, "I was somewhat surprised, actually. He seems intelligent in person, sometimes even articulate. You don't get that at all from his tortured, airport novelist prose."

Jane picked up Sarah's paperback copy of *The Delgado Cipher* and quickly leafed through its pages. "I haven't read this one, but if it's as bad as *The Faithful*, I'll skip it," Jane told Sarah, putting the book back down on Sarah's desk. "Carter Smith isn't just a hack - he's the king of the hacks! I'd never read such drivel."

Their editor, an older man who had been employed with *The Daily Sentinel* for many years, overheard the journalists' conversation on his way to his office. He stopped by Sarah's desk and interrupted them.

"You entirely miss the point, Ms. Roberts," the editor interjected. "Carter Smith's overrated drivel is targeted toward a certain species of reader: dullards, of which there are many." The editor then took a sip from his coffee cup and continued past the desk without waiting for a response.

Sarah reached for *The Delgado Cipher* paperback and opened the book to a random page, scanning it before looking over at Jane. "I tried to read some of Smith's earlier books before our interview: *The Forest*, *The Hills*, *The Tower*, and the one before *The Faithful*, titled *Them*. I struggled through the first few chapters of each one and ended up putting all of them down. The novels were so awful I just couldn't finish them.

"But *The Delgado Cipher*, it's almost as if it's written by a different person. Clear language, full descriptions, three-dimensional characters. And the symbolism, so complex that the novel really *could* contain a code of sorts." Sarah shut the paperback and looked up at Jane. "What's going on here? Do you think Bartleby & Bayne made him use a ghostwriter instead of just letting him become a washed-up has-been, drifting off into obscurity?"

Jane shrugged. "I couldn't say. Smith may have somehow found his artistic muse later in life. I know he lost his wife when he was younger. She went missing, and the case was never solved!" She made a face and stood, her hands held theatrically in the air. "Spooky, right?"

"He might finally be getting over her after all these years," Jane offered, a touch of sarcasm in her voice. "Maybe Carter Smith was an unpolished gem of a writer all along."

Carter pulled up in his convertible, maneuvering into a parking space along a quiet side street. The nearby coffee shop—his destination—was part of a major chain with locations across the country, and Carter ordered the same beverage every time he visited.

"A vanilla latte, large, extra hot," Carter told the barista behind the counter. "Yes, with foam. Thanks."

He took the hot paper cup in hand and seated himself on a stool behind the shop's open floor-to-ceiling window. Once settled, he began idly studying the strange mermaid illustration on the front of the paper cup, guessing the odd choice in company logo could, in fact, be an occult symbol.

Two nebbish young men, most likely college students, hesitantly approached Carter from a nearby table. "Mr.

Smith? Carter Smith?" the first man said, holding a paperback in his hands.

Carter turned around on his stool to face the pair, finishing his drink as he did so. "At your service. Is that *The Delgado Cipher*?" Carter pretended not to recognize a copy of his own novel.

"Oh, yes, Mr. Smith," the second man said, the two looking excitedly at each other. "We're your biggest fans. If you would, I'd like you to sign my book. This is the best story I've read in my life, sir." He opened to the title page beneath the book's front cover and held it out expectantly.

Carter began to search his shirt pocket for a pen, but the second man gave him one instead. "And who should I dedicate this to?" Carter asked, trying to be friendly.

"Please sign it, 'To Billy, my biggest fan. Carter Smith.'"

Carter wrote the dedication in a steady hand, returning the pen to its lender.

"I appreciate it so much, Mr. Carter," Billy said nervously. "We won't bother you anymore. We're both looking forward to your next novel." The pair looked at each other again and then walked away from Carter, picking up two backpacks at their table before leaving the coffee shop.

Carter returned to gazing out the shop's picture window. A young woman walked past who suddenly reminded him of his wife, Melissa. Uneasiness gripped him—he hadn't thought of Melissa for many years now. Why had he been reminded of her? The woman Carter had seen bore some resemblance to Melissa, but he had only taken a fleeting glance as she passed by.

There had been a small coffee shop and restaurant near his rented home in Avebury. He'd used to wake up late in the morning and then stroll along the village's narrow cobbled streets, ending his daily constitutional at the coffee shop with some breakfast scones and a cup of builder's tea.

DOORWAYS TO THE UNSEEN 2

One day, after more than a month of living in the village, Carter left the coffee shop and turned a corner along a backstreet. This was a different path than he usually took home, but he felt like taking the scenic route today.

As he walked, Carter noticed a cramped little shop on the other side of the tapered street, nestled in an alleyway. The shop's hanging sign read *Rare Books Emporium.* Odd— Carter had never seen the shop before, and it didn't look as if it had just opened.

Driven by curiosity, Carter ducked into the alleyway and opened the shop's door. A bell jingled somewhere overhead, and the musty smell of many old books greeted Carter's senses.

"And what might you be lookin' for on this fine day, young man?" A stooped figure, swathed in a gray sweater, stepped out from behind a standing shelf of books and stared directly at Carter. The old man's hair was long at the back, but his plate was mostly bald, making him seem unkempt and distracted.

"Good day to you," Carter said, a bit surprised by the shopkeeper's sudden appearance. "I'd just like to browse for a time if that's all right. Perhaps I'll find something once I look around." Carter noticed no other customers in the shop with them—though, actually, there wasn't much room for anyone else.

The shopkeeper adjusted the reading glasses above his nose and looked at Carter, as if studying him. "Are you a writer, then?" the old man said, the pitch of his voice falling somewhat.

"Ah, yes. But how would you have known that?" Carter was genuinely worried—there was something quite unnerving about this old man, as if he were somehow unreal.

"I know my trade, that is all," the shopkeeper replied, his voice becoming more relaxed. "After so many years in this business, I've dealt with a writer or two. Let me show you something."

The shopkeeper wheeled a rolling library ladder to a spot near the middle of a shelf. He climbed to the top and pulled a thick hardback book out from between a bunch of leather-bound tomes. This done, he clambered back down and presented the volume to Carter.

"This book is an English translation of a medieval Latin text. It contains numerology and even demonology," the shopkeeper said, his eyes squinting as he dusted the hardbound cover with a cloth. "The book also contains several stories which are believed, when read in succession, to conjure up the Devil."

"You must be mad! Why would I want such a book?" Carter was horrified, as if he had been offered something tainted with a deadly poison.

Undeterred, the old man continued, "The stories are masterworks, among the best written in any language. Those who read the stories will be inspired and are said to receive infernal guidance." The old man made a curious smile and placed the book into Carter's hands. "I will give this to you—as a gift."

The book was heavy and very aged, clearly an antique work. The shopkeeper wrapped it on the store's cluttered counter and then handed it back to Carter. Carter left without thanking him, a bell again jingling on his way out the door.

The shopkeeper pushed aside the white lace curtains of the bookshop window and watched Carter meander down the cobbled street outside. He wove and stumbled as he went, as if in an ecstatic daze.

Carter set the book on the writing desk of his cottage's study and began to carefully tear open its brown paper covering. The worn volume was tightly bound under its wrappings, tied together with burlap threads.

Opening the book, Carter took a deep breath and began to read the first story aloud in a quiet voice. The story told of the lord of a country manor who was very cruel and rapacious to everyone, including his own family. His subjects feared him and his capacity for viciousness. The lord sought great power, more than what his fiefdom could ever offer him, and so he made a pact with dark entities, entering into a bargain with them . . .

Carter sat at the writing desk of his home study, staring out at the garden. The late afternoon sun was just starting to dip behind the stately, manicured hedges, and small birds were settling in the treetops to roost. Shaking himself from his reverie, Carter rose and took a sturdy hardcover journal from the desk's drawer, opening it to a blank bookmarked page.

The Delgado Cipher had been written entirely in longhand, which had been something new for Carter. Previously, Carter had typed the drafts of every novel using word processing software, rarely making notes with a pencil or even revising much of what he had initially written.

After reciting the first story of the shopkeeper's book that day in Avebury, he'd taken some loose paper and written for hours without stopping. Carter wrote from the morning into the early evening, failing to notice he had missed meals or that the sun was beginning to set outside his cottage window. The first few draft chapters of *The Delgado Cipher* had been written in one sitting.

Afterward, Carter found that every time he began to write by hand, thoughts and words would come to him rapidly, his pen mysteriously guided by an unseen presence. What he wrote was also of a depth and maturity far beyond anything he had ever written before. Carter wept over the final draft of *The Delgado Cipher* once he read in full the words he had been impelled to transcribe.

His editor at Bartleby & Bayne was almost as surprised as Carter. "I'm not sure we can market this novel for you, Carter. Everything about this work is different; it's not your style at all except for its subject matter." Mr. Harold Raines sat across from Carter at his desk in the offices of Bartleby & Bayne, the draft copy of *The Delgado Cipher* resting in front of him.

"It's me, all right. I'm just a changed man, Harold." Carter was tired but relaxed, and he gratefully accepted the vanilla latte Mr. Raines' secretary brought him. "My time away from writing ripened the skills I've been developing throughout my career. This is my best novel yet. I'd bet my soul on it."

Mr. Raines didn't know whether to be amused by or worried about Carter. Carter Smith was a ham-fisted writer, and Bartleby & Bayne's editors knew it. However, the Carter Smith brand was also the most lucrative catalog at the publishing house; introducing this novel to his readers might not just confuse them, it might kill off Carter Smith's long-standing career as a popular novelist.

"I have to say, I was impressed by the manuscript," Mr. Raines said, putting his hands together at the fingertips as he spoke. "However, we'll have to have an internal dialogue before we decide to move forward with this project. I'll let you know soon."

Carter grinned as he recalled the successive months after *The Delgado Cipher*'s release. The shock at Bartleby & Bayne as *The Delgado Cipher* climbed the bestseller lists; the outpouring of enthusiasm from the writing community as Carter inexplicably gained some measure of legitimacy as a "real writer;" the acceptance, and even the excitement, from Carter's long-time fans of his new mode of writing.

Reaching into his desk drawer again, Carter produced the shopkeeper's book, a work with no title, author, or date.

He opened the book to the second story and began to read its words aloud, inhaling the scent of its moldering pages as he did so.

On the lands of the feudal lord was a monastery. The monastery's abbot was also corrupt and avaricious, presiding over his monks as a tyrant. The lord of the manor commissioned the abbot to direct one of his monastic scribes to write a book. The book was to be written on a particular paper, to illustrate specified depictions of both the holy and the fiendish, and to contain specific text, all in an assigned order. The instructions came not from the lord, but from his benefactor . . .

When Carter finally ceased writing, it was past midnight. He put his journal and the book back into the desk drawer and closed it for the night. He was exhausted but felt satisfied—after all, he'd made great progress. *The Possessed* would be another success, both commercial and critical. Carter believed he would leave a literary legacy behind him to be proud of with just a few more novels to his name.

He fell asleep quickly that night, despite being preoccupied with questions of his future. He had thought of Melissa earlier that day and didn't want to think of her again. Was what he did worth it, now that Carter's success was more enduring than just a hefty royalty check?

He dreamed of Melissa, of when they'd been young and in love. He dreamed of the terrible fights they'd had, of her threats to leave him and possibly end his fledgling writing career in the fallout of an acrimonious divorce.

"You spend so much time on your damn novels! I know we have to make a living, but . . ." Melissa trailed off, upset at yet again being ignored by Carter for days at a time. Carter had just received a substantial advance for his forthcoming book from Bartleby & Bayne, one which would allow him to write full-time finally.

"Melissa, you know I love you. But I'm on the cusp of something so big it could change our lives." Carter was afraid to show Melissa the check; she had already threatened to leave him on more than one occasion.

Melissa sighed in frustration. "It's just that we never go anywhere anymore. I feel so stifled. It's like I'm a prisoner in our apartment." She turned away from him, and he followed her, running a hand through her long, wavy tresses.

"We'll go somewhere, I promise. Very soon. I just need about another week to get this settled, and then I'll be free for a while." Carter felt the skin of Melissa's neck under his fingers. It was cold to the touch.

The next morning, Carter again took the journal from his writing desk drawer and held it open. He began reading through what he'd written the previous day but quickly stopped.

"I don't remember writing any of this," Carter thought to himself. There were entire pages, one after the other, with new characters, storylines, and sections of dialogue. The manuscript in the journal had been considerably expanded, with the novel's main story now interwoven with plots within plots. The overarching narrative of *The Possessed* was so grandiose in scope it surpassed even that of *The Delgado Cipher*.

Carter quickly closed the journal and put it back into the desk drawer, next to the shopkeeper's book. He was close to panic; the unholy inspiration he had felt before had troubled Carter, but this was entirely different. Someone or, more likely, *something* had written those words.

Warm summer winds whistled past Carter as he sped along the highway. He'd decided to break his morning writing ritual and take a ride in the convertible instead.

He wondered dimly what he should do with the bedeviled book. Without the book, Carter thought, he might never be able to write something like *The Delgado Cipher* again.

After a late lunch at a local eatery and a cruise around town, Carter returned home. When he arrived, he went straight to his study, where he opened the drawer and took out his journal, fearful of what he might find.

Yet more was written—much more. There was enough material here for a whole novel, though it appeared as if the story was not quite done. Carter sat and immersed himself in the mesmerizing tale, its account holding him rapt in attention.

As the light outside the study's window diminished, Carter realized how late in the day it had become. He put the journal into the drawer and then removed the book, opening its pages to the third story. This time, Carter's voice was only a whisper as he read the printed words.

The lord of the manor and the abbot both knew this illuminated manuscript would open an infernal portal, but the arc of the book's story had to first be resolved before the portal would open. Those who take part in the writing of the diabolical text are forever damned, their undying punishment fitting the crimes they may have committed in life. Even someone pure of heart still faced perdition, as they would be lost to God, the mark on their souls malignant for putting down the words of the Devil on paper.

Carter closed the cursed book and then held the journal with shaking hands. He took up his pen and wrote the last few pages of the story, its breathtaking, byzantine narrative reaching a preordained conclusion.

There was a glowing luminescence behind Carter, throwing shadows about the walls of the study now that night had fallen. He turned and gazed at the fiery aperture swelling behind him, torn into space itself. The ellipse-shaped rift emitted no heat, but its borders had the appearance of molten lava erupting from within the depths of the Earth.

Carter approached the aperture, staring into its gauzy center as the rift's boundaries bubbled and flowed. Figures seemed to move in the distance within its glimmering confines, trapped behind a translucent, hazy barrier.

The soil was tightly packed, so Carter dug quickly. Standing chest-deep in the makeshift grave, he threw another shovelful of dirt behind him, near Melissa's body. She had been dead for only a few hours, and Carter needed to finish before dark.

Carter had made sure no one knew where they had gone. Their trip into the countryside had been "a surprise," spontaneous. Carter and Melissa had left that day for the long drive upstate.

Their trip soon turned into another ugly argument. Carter knew Melissa was going to leave him, this time for good. They were alone in the woods when he began to feel his rage building, hating her for holding him back. He'd grasped the pointed shovel he had brought with them, its blade of hard steel . . .

An enormous black figure spread its cloak over Carter, swallowing him in front of his study's writing desk.

When the cloak parted, Carter was alone on a vast plane of night, its dark, smoldering sky menacing and streaked with falling spheres of fire. The cloaked figure stood off in the distance, the only thing visible against the foreboding backdrop.

Carter moved forward, pacing toward the featureless and silent entity, as if entranced. He drew closer, and the figure opened the folds of its cloak wide to reveal a woman. It was Melissa.

"Carter, my love. I forgive you. We can be together now, forever." Melissa stretched out her arms, as if to embrace her husband, the wounds on her corpse's face visible and ghastly. She ran toward Carter, and he turned and fled.

As the two lovers ran, the blasted landscape shifted and became the city street where they'd first met, the church in which they'd married, the town they had moved to after

Carter's first published novel, the woods where Carter had murdered Melissa...

Harold Raines laid the journal the police detective had found in Carter's study onto his office's desk. He still felt numb; he had never read such a fine, intricately detailed novel before. The book would be considered a classic of the genre once published—of that, he was absolutely sure.

If Carter ever resurfaced, his reputation as a newly flourishing master of fiction was ensured. But where the man could have been hiding was anyone's guess. The press had called it a publicity stunt, but no one at Bartleby & Bayne was complicit in such deceit. As far as Harold could tell, Carter had dropped off into oblivion.

The concluding line of *The Possessed* was what struck Harold most of all; even now, it would nudge its way into his head as he worked in his office or as he lay in bed at night. It read, "Nothing in this life is worth eternal damnation."

The shopkeeper parted the lace curtains of the store's front window, placing a hardcover book onto its display. The publisher's synopsis for the hardback edition of *The Possessed* exclaimed the novel was perhaps Carter Smith's final work, and the best of his career as an author.

About the Author

J ames Dermond is a writer who lives in Colorado. Intrigued from a very young age by horror anthologies and the short story form, he offers this book as his latest modest contribution to the genre.

Doorways to the Unseen 2: 6 Tales of Terror and Suspense is the second volume in a series of short story collections, of which twelves volumes are planned.

To sign up for free eBooks and other future giveaways, please subscribe to James Dermond's author website here: www.jamesdermond.com

James Dermond's Amazon Page
https://www.amazon.com/James-Dermond/e/B01M1S54YP

James Dermond's Goodreads Page
https://www.goodreads.com/author/show/15862747.James_Dermond

James Dermond on Facebook
https://www.facebook.com/JamesDermondAuthor/

James Dermond on Twitter
https://twitter.com/JamesDermond

Postscript

Thank you for reading this latest volume in the short horror story series, Doorways to the Unseen! We are now on volume two of what will eventually become a twelve-volume series of books.

I conceived of this series as an effort to help revive the short horror story format, which has become somewhat neglected since its heyday during the 19th century and early 20th century. Authors such as Edgar Allan Poe, Ambrose Bierce, Arthur Machen, M.R. James, and H.P. Lovecraft were all essential in shaping the horror fiction genre as it exists today. However, relatively few authors now write in the aforementioned literary luminaries' style or focus primarily on their favored medium: the short story. The Doorways to the Unseen series will continue to explore the themes and tropes of those writers' works and those of similar authors, as well as introduce short stories whose sources of inspiration are, I hope, entirely new.

From television, early horror anthology series have also inspired the stories in Doorways to the Unseen. Shows such as *One Step Beyond* (1959-1961), *Night Gallery* (1969-1973), *Hammer House of Horror* (1980), *Darkroom* (1981-1982), and *Tales from the Darkside* (1983–1988) have influenced some of the stories planned or already published in this series, however subtly. The influence of full-length movie horror anthologies like *Dead of Night* (1945), *Black Sabbath* (1963), *Asylum* (1972), *The Vault of Horror* (1973), and *Trilogy of Terror* (1975) on this short story series could not be understated.

The horror genre has thrilled and terrified its readers and viewers for two centuries now, offering an escape from the ordinary but also delving into the most primal and subconscious places in the human mind. No other form of fiction can so effectively tap into the most visceral emotions of its readers, abruptly bringing to the surface submerged phobias and past terrors hitherto long buried. And no other form of fiction can so fluidly blend genres and take the reader out of their circumstance, especially into the unexpected. As Lovecraft noted at the onset of his essay, "Supernatural Horror in Literature" (1927), "The oldest and strongest emotion of mankind is fear, and the oldest and strongest kind of fear is fear of the unknown."

The first horror novel could be considered Horace Walpole's *The Castle of Otranto* (1764), the Gothic tale of a young woman trapped in a castle with its lord who wants to marry her. Walpole's novel was part of a larger Gothic literary movement that subsequently gained momentum and became the horror fiction genre in the 19th century. With the publication of Mary Shelley's novel *Frankenstein* (1818), the beginnings of the horror genre as we now know it were established. But the roots of horror stretch back as far as a millennium or longer, to the folklore and religious traditions of medieval societies, and even before that period.

The Doorways to the Unseen series intends to journey back to this earlier time near the origins of the horror genre, making what may have been forgotten by many remembered again. So, step inside and find that which has been hidden from you all along. Where the unknown and the unimaginable meet.

If you enjoyed this collection of stories, please leave a review on Amazon and other online bookstores where volumes in the Doorways to the Unseen series can be found. A positive review will help promote the book and inform other readers of the book's merits.

www.ingramcontent.com/pod-product-compliance
Lightning Source LLC
Chambersburg PA
CBHW020422130626
46549CB00006B/2701